RED ROCK

RED ROCK

a mystery

Wayne Tefs

COTEAU BOOKS

Thanks to David Arnason, James Hutchison, and Geoffrey Ursell.

Edited by Geoffrey Ursell.

Cover painting, "The Enigma of Iron," by Iris Hauser.
Cover design by Ed Pas.
Book design by Duncan Campbell.
Printed and bound in Canada.

The publisher gratefully acknowledges the financial assistance of the Saskatchewan Arts Board, the Canada Council for the Arts, the Department of Canadian Heritage, and the City of Regina Arts Commission, for its publishing program.

Coteau Books celebrates the 50th Anniversary of the Saskatchewan Arts Board with this publication.

Canadian Cataloguing in Publication Data

Tefs, Wayne, 1947-
Red rock
ISBN 1-55050-135-6

1. Title.

PS8589.E37R43 1998 C813'.54 C98-920119-8
PR9199.3.T4R43 1998

COTEAU BOOKS
401-2206 Dewdney Ave.
Regina, Saskatchewan
Canada S4R 1H3

AVAILABLE IN THE US FROM
General Distribution Services
85 River Rock Drive, Suite 202
Buffalo, New York, USA 14207

for Kristen and Andrew

Then you must speak
Of one that loved not wisely, but too well;
Of one not easily jealous, but being wrought,
Perplex'd in the extreme.

– *Othello*

Northwest Ontario, 1963

Graveyard

Andy Buechler:

Hank Peterson went into the bedroom of his house one Friday morning about 6:30, carrying a shotgun, and when he came out the lives of everyone in Red Rock had changed forever. It was Hank who was affected most: and Becky, his wife; and their son, Scott. And Tommy Piper, who was the man inside the bedroom when Hank walked in with the shotgun.

It was all about sex, said Gordy McCabe.

It was fall and Hank had driven home early from work, taking his car out of gear at the top of Spruce Road and letting it drift in the shadows of dawn past the houses where fathers and mothers were shuffling about in robes, making coffee and watering plants. I heard the car motor through the window. I was up having a pee and drew aside the curtain in the bathroom to see what was going on. Hank and Becky

Peterson lived next door to us. His car was a nearly-new Meteor, the tires caked red with clay from the iron mines where he worked. The Meteor came to rest against the curb, a puff of exhaust billowing out of the tail pipe. I saw Hank through the windshield. I rubbed the sandman from my eyes. Hank sat there a moment, hands on the steering wheel, as if unsure whether or not he was going to get out, and I imagined he might suspect I was spying on him, so I closed the curtain and flushed the toilet.

If I'd watched I would have seen him take the shotgun out of the back seat, would have seen him go up the front steps, to kill his wife and her lover.

It was all about sex, Gordy said, all about the beast with two backs. That was Gordy McCabe, my pal.

My old man said it had more to do with the stuff going on at the mine, the fights and picket lines and scabs. Tempers were running high. I'd heard Hank say as much himself.

Hank Peterson was in his late twenties, a stocky man who had a spring in his step and a ready smile on his face. He pushed his dark hair up on top and into a duck's ass in back, the hard-rock look that went with the open-neck shirt and stand-up collar. Like most of the kids in Red Rock I knew Hank because he coached our teams – in winter hockey, in summer baseball. During the hockey season Hank played for the Red Rock MineKings, our senior team. On summer evenings I'd see him in his backyard shirtless, hauling dirt from one corner of his property to another. The muscles of Hank's torso rippled as he worked.

He had a tattoo of a green snake curled around a red rose stem on the bicep of one arm and it made him look tough, which he could be.

That was the fall there was a wildcat strike at the mines. For a year or more the companies had been bringing in earth haulers to replace the Euclid trucks that carted the raw iron from the pits to the rail cars, which then took it on to the smelting cities of the Great Lakes for processing. The trucks carried thirty-five tons of ore but the earth haulers carted over a hundred, so the union was dead against them. The *Red Rock Record* reported the men were ready to go out on strike, no matter how negotiations went between the company and the union, because the earth haulers threatened to take away the livelihoods of so many union members.

The machines themselves were awe-inspiring. They were painted the colour of mustard and belched huge clouds of black diesel smoke into the air. You felt dwarfed beside them. The wheels were so big a kid could stand inside them, feet on the bottom lip of the rim, head not touching the upper one.

Hank did not drive one of the impressive earth haulers. In Red Rock they did two types of mining, underground and open pit. The men working underground were carried down to the ore in steel cage elevators that clanked and lurched and often did not run at all. Underground it was hot, filthy and brutal work, labouring in claustrophobic spaces to wrest the ore from the earth, often a dozen men labouring in a space hardly bigger than a washroom. Water stood knee deep in the rectangular tunnels where the men dug and picked in the ore during eight-hour shifts. Breathing was difficult, and vision too. There was a lot of dust. Tools fell on the miners' feet. From time to time one of the mine shafts collapsed.

Hank worked in the open pit above ground, a labourer, a grunt. He was on one of the blasting crews, operating a drill that he held on his shoulder to bore into the rock face so that the blasting foreman could set charges and break up the rock face. It was dangerous work. Sometimes charges went off before they should have. By the end of a shift Hank's clothes were covered in black muck and red dust. During the summer they were dry, but when it rained and all through the winter when the crew shovelled away the new-fallen snow, his boots, pants, and shirts were caked with mud and slag. It was impossible to remove the red dirt from under the nails, no matter how long a man spent scrubbing at the sink. It thickened the men's hair and got into their ears and nostrils. It became a stain that would be just nicely fading away when they returned from their two week vacations in the summer.

Hank was one of the men whose jobs was in jeopardy, since jobs in the union went by seniority and he was a relative newcomer to the mines. He was not happy about that.

One night he and Father exchanged words about

the whole business standing in their backyards. When we were in the house afterward Father said to Mother, "You see what I mean." I was in the darkened hallway on my way to bed. Father added, "First the men belly ache about their pay and threaten to go out on strike, and then when the companies bring in conveyor belts so they won't have to deal with strikes, the men threaten to vandalise the machines."

Mother was at the kitchen counter and Father was standing beside her near the sink. She said, "I hate it when the men are at each other's throats this way. It makes me sick to the stomach."

"If they go out on strike our business will be cut in half."

Mother sighed and clattered flatware in the sink. "No one ever thinks of that," she said. "It's always union this and company that, but no one ever says anything about the small businesses that keep this town afloat."

Father said, "This afternoon, Hank tells me, a couple of the men took pipe wrenches to Sam Johnson's car. Smashed out the headlights and the windshield on the Edsel before the security guys knew anything was going on."

"Roy," Mother said, "that's against the law, attacking private property."

"So now the company has armed guards posted at the gates checking the miners as they come out, lunch pails and everything."

"They'll lose their jobs, they could go to jail."

"There were punch-ups. Some of the men refused to be searched."

"I hate this, Roy, every one in town taking up sides."

"I know. Hank took a swing at somebody. Cecil Werner."

"He's a foreman, right?"

"Yes, big man. That's not the worst. Hank is pissed off at me now."

"Roy, you be careful. Hank's a lot younger than you. He has a temper. They say he was on the mine road the day that young cop got stabbed. Lee."

"I can take care of myself."

"And he's a miner, Hank is, so he sees things in black and white when it comes to the union. He could attack you. Don't all the miners carry knives?"

"What am I supposed to do? Say nothing? I'm entitled to my views."

"You can show a little discretion. For the sake of your family."

Father grunted. His views on miners included the phrases *layabouts* and *goldbricks.* But he bit his tongue and said, "So now Becky takes the kid over to the Johnsons for Sunday supper and Hank heats himself up a pork chop."

"You see what I mean," Mother said, "families divided. It's ugly."

"Sam Johnson would like to see Hank run out of town." Father paused and then added, "And Becky doesn't help, tramping around the way she does."

"Roy," Mother said, "not that again."

"According to Dixon...."

"Hush," Mother said. "No more, Roy."

"The way she dresses, those skirts, she's asking for it, she's...."

"No more." After a pause Mother added, "I think you're sore because Hank and you had a fight about unions."

"It was not a fight. We were discussing."

"I heard what he said about you. That was uncalled for."

"He's angry and he's young, young men talk that way in the heat of the –"

"They do not call their neighbours *assholes.*"

"Anyway, I'm only saying about Becky...."

"I know what you're saying. And it's ugly."

Father cleared his throat. "She spreads her legs," he said, "is the talk."

"Men. Men talk like that." There was a pause and then Mother added, "It's ugly talk. Becky doesn't deserve it. Hank neither. It's beneath them – us."

Father stroked his jaw. Because he had to get up so early in the morning he shaved at night. At the dinner table he smelled of Fitchy's Rose Water. "At least he's not a weasel," Father said, "like some I could name around here."

Mother clucked her tongue. "Roy," she said.

"You know who I mean. A weasel with a woody pecker."

"Leave it be," she said.

Father snorted. "You watch. One of these nights Hank's pals are going to grab that Tommy coming out of the Rockland and teach him a lesson."

"Wonderful. Then the town really will be in two camps. Like a war."

"It's what he deserves," Father said, "the slimy little weasel."

There was no more talk between Hank and Father about unions and strikes after that one night. Hank still whistled as he worked in his backyard that fall or played with Scott, his two-year-old son, but maybe underneath he was boiling. Something has to explain that shotgun and what he did to Tommy Piper and Becky – doesn't it?

She was a terrier, high strung and constantly darting about the way small dogs do – in and out of the house, banging the screen door shut behind her the way Mother scolded us for doing. She spoke herky-jerky, too, jumping from one topic of conversation to another. "Beats me," she'd say with a shrug when she and Mother were gossiping. Or ask, "You serious, kiddo?" She smoked cigarettes, puffing absent-mindedly. I don't reckon she liked smoking as much as the idea of smoking, the way it fitted with an image she had of herself from the movies she and Hank went to see at the Red Rock Theatre when they left Scott with Kelly Spelchak – who was in the same grade at Red Rock High as me. Becky stubbed out each cigarette half-smoked. She messed with her hair as she talked, tugging a curl over one ear, or flicking the bang on her forehead.

Becky had been Rebecca Johnson before she married Hank. Her father was a big shot at the mine and her parents lived in a three-storey house on Birch Crescent, where the Hancock twins lived and Gordy McCabe. Those houses sat on the hill and looked down on the rest of Red Rock. Gordy was my best pal, despite the fact that as high school students we were supposed to be beyond that sort of thing – and the fact his father was the town doctor while mine ran a laundry business.

Hank wasn't a local boy. He'd been a teacher in Toronto before coming to Red Rock. That hadn't worked out, he told me, because he liked kids but was forced to yell and scold and threaten. "Playing policeman," he confided to me, "brought out the worst in my character." The way he said it, I had the impression maybe he'd lost control of himself and hit a kid or something.

As a coach he was okay. On the hockey rink he taught us the tricks of winning face-offs and how to throw a hip check. "It's all timing," he explained, waiting until the precise second when the puck carrier thinks he's got you beat before dropping your shoulder and catching him in mid-stride. "That's when you nail him," Hank said. He did not shy away from violence. If somebody bothers a team mate, he said, you leap to his defense. You want to get your shots in early, aim for the nose, when you hit a man in the nose his eyes tear over and then you can really smash in his face. "Hit hard and hit often. You bust his nose up, he won't bother you any more, by the Christ."

It thrilled me to hear Hank talk that way – swearing almost. Sometimes he'd yell at us, "Get out there you bums and give 'er dogwater." Nobody knew what that meant, *dogwater*, but it was fun to repeat, and we found ourselves saying it in the changing room as we dressed or on the bench in mid-game. Talking like that, like men, loosened us up and made playing the games fun.

Of course there was that time with Randy Waltin. He was a jerk, Randy, he picked on younger kids and made it obvious he had no time for grown-ups. One day at practice Hank was explaining something to us and Randy was, as usual, mouthing off in the background. Hank had told him to shut up before. You could see it bothered Hank. He glared over once or twice and the next time Randy laughed out loud again Hank took two quick steps across to him, grabbed him by the scruff of the neck, and shoved him up against the boards. Randy's helmet fell off. "Enough!" Hank said between gritted teeth. No one laughed then. The next day Hank apologized to the whole team. "I lost it," he said, "I lost my temper." We all looked at the ground until Hank said, "Okay, let's give 'er dogwater, guys," and that was the end of that.

His wife Becky didn't have a lot to do with us kids. When she wasn't looking after Scott, she worked as a nurse at the Red Rock General, so she was coming and going at odd hours. At home, she spent most of her time indoors. I'd catch a glimpse of her through the windows sometimes, walking around in a dressing gown, a cig in one hand, a magazine in the other, smoke forming a kind of scarf around her head. It was thrilling to see a woman like that – naked almost, and flaunting it. She played records, too, at high volume, Perry Como and Frank Sinatra, moony stuff, nothing like Elvis, but sexy all the same. Sometimes she would dance by herself, and once, maybe sensing that someone was watching her, she did a strip-tease sort of thing, flinging off items of clothing as she sashayed around the living-room. My throat went dry. I was watching from my bedroom window, and I stayed there, fascinated, for what seemed like an hour, until I had to relieve myself, so to speak. What Gordy called "choking the Bishop."

I don't reckon Becky liked kids, but then she didn't like many things. She called Red Rock a *dump* and a *hole* when she and Mother gossiped, and when she really got going *godforsaken hole.* I couldn't understand why anyone wouldn't like Red Rock. The Theatre showed "Rebel Without A Cause" and "East of Eden" and I saw them both three times. The high school had recently been completed – and there was talk of a highway being built west through the shield to Fort Frances and then on to Winnipeg. The Red Rock MineKings had travelled to Trail, BC, the winter before to contest the Allan Cup.

Maybe it wasn't these things Becky had in mind when she called Red Rock a dump. She'd come out into the yard to talk to Hank at night when he was planting spruces along the back of their property. She'd have her hands on her hips and a cig smouldering between her fingers, and Hank would be nodding as she spoke and he dug in the unyielding earth of the shield. Becky wore tight and short skirts and was partial to angora sweaters – which flattered her breasts. Gordy McCabe called her a dish. "I wouldn't throw her out of bed for eating crackers," he said, repeating something the older guys in the locker room sometimes said. When Becky came out on those nights, she would talk to Hank while he was planting, their voices hushed and strained. You could tell from the way she scuffed her feet after a few minutes that she was trying to get him to do something, but whatever she said things always ended up the same way – Becky would stamp one foot and then wheel away from Hank suddenly, and he'd stand for a moment pushing at his hair before going back to his work. A few minutes later we'd hear the clicking of heels on the sidewalk and the car door slamming before Becky sped off.

"She's hot as a pistol," Gordy McCabe said. I looked at him funny and he said, "She's begging for it, but Hank is happy planting trees and digging in the dirt and looking after the kid. He's a yo-yo. He's going to lose that girl if he's not careful."

Another time she actually hit him. He was bending over, grunting, not really listening to what she was saying, so she punched him in the shoulder, a girl punch, more to get his attention than anything else. Hank hardly flinched. "Don't try that again," he said without looking up. "I don't want to hurt you." He raised one hand and waved her away. His hands were broken and gnarled, as if they'd been caught in machinery and had not healed properly, the hands of a tough. Gordy and I were just within hearing range.

"My God," I said, "you think he would do that, smack his wife?"

"Hot pants," said Gordy, "just a-going to waste."

One evening we were outside playing catch when Becky crossed the yard to talk to Hank. It was just at sunset, the last slanting rays of light playing in Becky's hair as she strode past in a tight-fitting skirt. I guess she'd put the baby to bed already or called Kelly Spelchak in to sit him because she seemed ready for a night on the town. "Hi, boys," she called over the fence, waving her cig in our direction. The smell of perfume wafted toward us.

Gordy came over and stood beside me. "Buster," he whispered, "you would not kick her out of bed for shedding hair."

Hank was shovelling horse manure into holes that he'd dug for planting spruces. As usual, Becky stood in front of Hank on the grass. We heard her say, *sometimes just sometimes.* Then she threw her cigarette on the ground. She shouted, *listen to me!* Hank did not say anything but he stepped close to her and hit her in the mouth with the open palm of his hand. Then she made a mewling sound, a hurt cat sound, and sat down right beside Hank in the horse dung. Her skirt had ridden up her thighs. Her hands were flat in her lap and her feet splayed out in front, like a doll abandoned in the middle of play. Hank dropped beside her, holding his head in both hands and rocking back and forth while he moaned her name. It went on for about half an hour. She sat there in the growing darkness, feet stuck straight out front long after Mother had called us in for Cokes.

As we put our ball gloves away Gordy said, "No more nooky there."

That night I realized how difficult it was to be an adult. Seeing Becky sitting stiff-legged on the grass with Hank crouched beside her frightened me. Both of them seemed so small and helpless in the face of whatever it was that had brought her to plunk herself down in the horse dung like that. But it was clear their lives were out of control, somehow, in a small but terrifying way. I was happy to retreat indoors for a Coke and the meaningless but comforting chatter of my parents. At sixteen there were things I did not want to know about the world, things I was afraid of but couldn't admit to and wouldn't have known how to deal with even if I could have admitted to them.

I don't know how long Becky Peterson sat out in the horse manure that night. Mother made Gordy leave through the front door when we were done drinking our Cokes – and it was too dark to see anything in

Hank's yard when I looked through my bedroom window later. I didn't hear anything either, but I stayed up late listening to Dick Biondi on WLS, the Chicago station our radios picked up nights despite the static thrown up by the iron in the hills around Red Rock. Humming along to Little Richard and the Diamonds on the glowing little radio beside my bed, I thought about how rigid Becky's body became after she'd been sitting for a few minutes in the yard and how desperate Hank had looked as he crouched beside her. I was sorry for both of them and glad I was not an adult – glad but not happy.

I went for a walk that night, long past the time when my parents were asleep and I was supposed to be too. I slipped out of the house and climbed up the hill in the centre of Red Rock – the hill where the town council had erected the siren that signalled noon every day. I hadn't been up there for years. From the top of the hill you saw the whole town: the blinking pink neon sign of the Steep Rock Café; the Pickerel River snaking through the middle of Red Rock, dividing the poor from the wealthy, the collapsing shacks of Front Street on one side, the imposing brick houses of Birch Crescent on the other; the high school; the yellow glow of the lights from the mines in the distance. At night you heard the rumble of machines, the steady growl of earth haulers punctuated from time to time by the wheezing of conveyor belts. It was enough to make you feel sad and lonely standing up there any time, but I felt especially lonely that chilly fall night with winter coming on.

I realized something important had happened, but I wasn't sure what or where it would lead next. Everything seemed off centre: Hank hitting his wife, the sounds Becky made, the fact little Scottie was alone in his crib while his parents fought outside. When he'd left our house Gordy McCabe had said, "Tits up." He meant Hank and Becky.

Hours later I stood in the cold air still puzzling it through. I wanted to get things straight in my head, but I knew wanting to and being able to were two different matters. Was sex so important it could turn you violent? Hank had crossed over some line that even Tommy hadn't.

It was cold on the hilltop, and I watched the ghosts of my breath drift overhead. Soon it would snow. Below me I saw the headlights of cars weaving along the streets of Red Rock. Horns bleating, tires squealing. There was movement on the parking lot of the Rockland Hotel – closing time, maybe – and the sounds of doors banging and shouted voices. After a while my eyes picked out a semi-trailer pulling away from the Safeway across from Father's laundry where I worked in the summer, sorting and folding the miners' socks and shirts. I could hear the driver picking up speed from the way the engine chuffed every few seconds and then re-caught as he shifted gears. I followed the sound down Main Street and over the bridge that crossed the Pickerel River, and then I lost it when the truck went behind the granite hills marking the edge of town.

I had a premonition Hank would leave Red Rock on that road soon, packing his things into the Meteor one morning and driving away in a swirl of red dust. I wondered where he would go and what he would do. He'd talked about the DEW line one time: "The north is the last frontier." He had a notion you could make so much money there you could set yourself up for life. It was more likely he would just get in more trouble and die regretting he hadn't been able to hang on to Becky.

I'd come out that night seeking clarity, but the more I thought about things the more muddled I became. If lust got the better of men and women, then what did control mean? Father had always said *Be the boss, Be the guy in charge.* He'd bought his own business in Red Rock so he could be in charge of his life, and ours, and I'd taken in the idea around the kitchen table, along with the corn flakes and chicken noodle soup: *Be in charge of your own life: not just the obvious stuff, but the spiritual side, too.* That's why Hank Peterson scared me. As good a man as he was, Hank had lost control of his inner self when he struck Becky, and if Hank could lose control that way, then who would not?

An owl hooted in the bushes behind me, and when I looked over my shoulder I saw a huge white moon, cold and bright, craters and cliffs distinctly visible. It had never seemed that close to earth before, almost within reach – it frightened me and I stepped back awkwardly, losing my footing. It seemed to me that the ground had given way suddenly – ridiculous, but real as grass. For a moment I had the sensation that my head was floating way above the earth, fifty feet or more, and then everything righted itself.

I was trembling, but not from the cold, yet I didn't know why either, because nothing very important had happened. Hank had hit his wife and she had sat in a pile of horse manure and I had felt the bottom go out of my life. I realized then I had thought what I'd come out to understand was about Hank, but it wasn't. It was about me. I'd put my trust in something – in Hank – and now I saw it would not hold up. No, it wasn't that, it was bigger than Hank – not him so much as the fact I wasn't sure I could ever trust anything again – or anyone.

Below me the town looked ghostly. A few car motors thrummed in the business section and then everything was silent. Silent and cold. I'd spent my formative years here, but Red Rock didn't seem like home to me anymore. I waited until my knees stopped trembling and the ground felt solid beneath my feet again. I hugged my arms about my body and made my way back into town and the warm bed awaiting me there.

Hank never said anything about that night, but it must have bothered him more than he let on. For a couple of weeks he spent less time in the backyard shifting dirt. We didn't see very much of him. Some nights he and Becky went out wearing dress clothes, Becky with her hair up and Hank in a blazer with a handkerchief tucked into the breast pocket. They were handsome. In the right light Becky looked like Natalie Wood. Mother said they went dancing at the Flame Club. Father grunted from behind the *Free Press*.

There was already talk around Red Rock about Becky, even us kids had heard her referred to as a *tramp* by the cheapest girls in the senior grades, and Father was expressing his disapproval in the only way he knew how. Mother told us to ignore what people whispered behind the Petersons' backs: that Becky went alone to parties at the Rock-a-Bye Motel and didn't get back until just before Hank arrived home from the graveyard shift; that Becky had been seen driving around in Tommy Piper's car.

"She's shacked up with a different guy every weekend and dopey old Hank thinks she's doing night shift at the Red Rock General," Gordy McCabe sneered over Cokes one night as we listened to "That's All Right" and "Rip It Up" on his record player. We couldn't imagine anyone more outrageous than Elvis Presley – or exciting. "She's shacked up this very minute with some lucky stiff," Gordy added, suggesting as he raised his eyebrows that he wouldn't mind if it were him.

That sort of talk made my blood run cold, and not just because the idea of going to bed with Hank's wife – however exciting on one level – seemed a monstrous betrayal after all he'd done for us. For me. I didn't say anything. Arguing with Gordy about

Hank was useless, and I had vowed not to reveal what I had seen a few nights earlier at the Petersons'. Maybe I cared for Hank so much I didn't want to see him hurt, even if it was only by talk. I wanted to protect him from the gossip of Gordy McCabe and people like him – the rumour mongers slavering to hear I'd seen Tommy Piper's Chevy parked behind the shack at the skating rink when I came home after the midnight show at the Red Rock Theatre on Saturday night. All the lights were off at the Petersons' save one, the bedroom.

Gordy said, referring to Becky, "That's *night shift* all right."

We both laughed, thinking about how dangerous sex was and how close we were to it ourselves. I'm not just talking about the medical textbook Gordy got hold of one time from his father's library. Guys on the hockey team talked about condoms and blow jobs and one of them asked me point blank once if I'd got my finger wet yet. I felt uneasy about talk like that, but excited too.

It didn't help that we lived next door to Becky Peterson and that I was always being tempted by the dancing silhouettes behind those white gauze curtains. I did wonder why it was that Tommy Piper had a thing for Becky when there were so many good-looking women around Red Rock he could have had for the asking. It was a question I tried out on Gordy, and he looked at me and said, "Don't you understand anything?" I had to admit I didn't understand much beyond wrist shots and dishing out hip checks – things I did well, to be fair to myself. Maybe that was Hank's problem too. "It's the old glands," Gordy said. "Thinking with your dick instead of your brain."

That was Tommy Piper in a nutshell. He wore blobs of Brylcream in his swooped-up hair and always had a cig in his lips, which the girls thought sexy. He drove a red Chevy with a coon tail tied to the radio aerial. I only ever heard him say one thing, and that was as he drove away from The Steep Rock Café, tires screeching. He shouted back to two other men who'd jumped out of the car while it was still rolling, "No sloppy seconds for this cowboy." All three men laughed, and Tommy waved as he wheeled the car around the corner and disappeared from sight. I agreed with Gordy that this was a man driven by lust. It upset me, though. But I was learning to look at things in a different way, a way I didn't always feel good about, a way that made me like myself a little less than I had before – an adult's way.

It was certainly an adult who told Hank about Becky and Tommy Piper, some jerk with a grudge against him or Becky or Tommy – or all three.

Whoever it was, Hank found out.

In Red Rock almost everyone owned a gun. The bushes of the shield were loaded with spruce grouse that anyone could bag on a Saturday afternoon jaunt. If you were walking near the edge of town you could hear the muffled discharges coming from the bushes – *whump, whump*. Most of the kids I went to school with owned their own .22s and roamed the woods around town on weekends and summer vacations, murdering birds and whatever else happened across our paths. There were moose, too, for serious hunters with rifles and skinning knives. Even my father, who detested weapons after his experiences in Europe, bought an over-and-under shotgun that we potted around with in the underbrush several times every year.

I knew Hank Peterson owned a shotgun and a rifle. For a couple years we'd talked about going on a hunting expedition during moose season one fall soon, and even if neither of us expected that talk to lead to anything as specific as dates and times, it was pleasant to while away the hours imagining where we might go and for how long. His rifle was a pump-style Winchester. He showed it to me one time and let me work the action. When I expressed my admiration, Hank said he preferred the shotgun – not quite so clean a kill but more effective.

The rumour around town that summer was that every miner was carrying a rifle in the trunk of his car in case anything explosive happened at the mines. All through July and August the union had been negotiating with the companies about layoffs, but the earth haulers kept rolling into town, so it was obvious that the layoffs would continue. The *Red Rock Record* said that more than a dozen earth haulers would be operating in the pits by the end of summer. The talk in the Union Hall, according to Hank, was at fever pitch. Most of the miners wanted to go out on wildcat. Then one afternoon there was a fight on the road to the mines between a gang of drivers from the day shift and the men going in to operate the earth haulers at night. Nobody had been hurt badly, but there had been fist fights, and guns had come out before the police arrived and talked everybody down. Hank had a bruise the size of a hockey puck over one eye. He confided to me, "There's some grudges festering pretty good already."

Mother said, "This is getting serious, Roy. I'm afraid for the kids."

"Yes," he said. This was after dinner when my sisters and I washed up.

"Somebody said there was guns and shooting."

"No," Father said. "They had it out on the mine road today, union guys on one side, the wildcat crowd on the other. A punch up. Terry Russell got his nose broken and now the whole Russell clan is laying for Cecil Werner."

"My god," said Mother. "What does that mean *laying for?"*

"It means they're going to pay him back."

Mother was putting food into the refrigerator. "Cecil Werner, wasn't he the one who got stabbed last year?"

"That was his brother," Father said. "Daryl."

"Daryl, Cecil, who named those Werners?"

"Daryl was the one got stabbed."

"They said he nearly died from those wounds. Lost a kidney."

"I never had much time for the Werners."

"That's hardly the point," Mother said.

"Hank says they carry knives, they come at a man from behind."

"Grown men prowling the streets with knives and guns, that's the point."

"Hank says they were close at hand when young Dave Lee was killed."

"What about their families, what about innocent kids?"

"We'll have to keep the kids close to home for a while. Off the mine road for sure. And away from the Rockland Hotel."

"Maybe send them to Mother's. If it gets worse."

"Maybe. But Dixon says it won't."

"A town cop," Mother said. "What would he know?"

By late September the RCMP detachment had been moved into town to help the town cops. There was talk that one company was going to replace the drivers operating the Euclids in the open pits with a three-mile long conveyor belt that would transport ore from the pits directly to the rail cars, by-passing the need for drivers. No one knew how many jobs would be lost then, but no one was optimistic either. Hank said as many as five hundred men might be out of work by spring. Like Father, he was touchy at the end of the working day. Over dinner Father often looked pre-occupied and Mother shooed us out of the house as soon as the dishes were done so they could talk.

One night I heard her say, "If they go out on strike we lose it all?"

Father was drinking rye and water at the kitchen table and had his shirt sleeves rolled up to the elbow. "The men are itching to go out. They want a show-down. They want a blood bath."

"Already everyone is walking on egg shells at Eaton's."

"They're just looking for an excuse, the men, to get violent."

"Muriel McCarthy goes to The Hudson Bay now where all the bosses' wives go. Even though she's a local girl. Somebody said something to her last week, some ugly thing, imagine that, Roy, it's not the women's fight."

"It's everyone's fight. Muriel is against Myrtle, Sam is against Hank."

"Even us? You've been threatened?"

"We were close to a punch up, that night, me and Hank."

"Oh Lord, Roy. I'd like to just up and move out of here."

Father snorted. "I'm not married to this town."

"No, only to me." Mother laughed and Father too.

"It's going to end in something bad," Father said,

"you watch. Someone is going to get killed before this is over. Tempers are at fever pitch, I saw that in the war. The men want a showdown, they want blood. It's infectious."

There was only strained silence for a minute, and then Mother said, "We never should have come to this town. Blood red dirt you can't wash away."

Father sighed. "Don't start up again."

"I've got friends, I know people in the city," Mother said. "I can get a job at Eaton's or working in the market."

"No," Father said.

"I'm not standing by watching my kids get maimed because some blood-crazed miners are at each other's throats."

Hank Peterson must have been a little blood-crazed when he booked off early at the mine that morning. He'd been working graveyard shift for nearly two weeks and that can turn a man strange in the head all on its own – sleeping when everyone else in town is working, eating meals at the wrong time of day, your whole system out of whack with what it's used to and what everyone else is doing. Scores of miners on graveyard shift couldn't take it. Most suffered constipation or migraine headaches or turned to alcohol to numb the effects. "You don't know whether to shit or jump through a window," Hank told me, trying to explain the weird effect that turning your whole day upside down had on you. It was no wonder that every winter some miner committed suicide when he got home from graveyard shift, usually with a rifle.

Hank had the shotgun in the back seat of the Meteor, and a mickey of rye up front. I had flushed the toilet and was already back in the bedroom when we heard the shots. The first one took me by surprise. I wasn't certain for a minute I'd really heard a shot. But there was no mistaking that sound – *blam.* It was loud. It rattled the windows in their panes. I sat up in bed and looked at the window a moment, as if waiting for confirmation. My heart was pounding in my chest. Then the sound came again, *blam,* just the same as the first time, only muffled somewhat. I heard Father say something to Mother and then the clatter of his shoes going down the back steps in a hurry. Running. "Be careful," Mother called after him. In a minute I was out of bed, looking through the window just in time to see Father run around to the front of the Petersons' house, an outline in the shadowy light of dawn. He was carrying something white that flapped as he ran.

I wasn't dressed and I made a mad scramble for my clothes. The sound of that second shot, more than a repetition of the earlier one, an echo, rang in my ears. It meant something serious, deadly serious, was going on.

Mother shouted at me, "Andy, stay here." And when the door banged behind me, "Stay away from that house, Andrew."

I started for the back door, but then I saw Father through the window with his hands on Hank's shoulders and changed my mind. I stopped on the grass and stood on my toes, peering into the window at them. There was a light on in the hallway of the Petersons' house, but even though I was nearly six feet tall, I couldn't see anything except their heads and shoulders. Hank was standing in the centre of the room. Father seemed to be talking in that intense way adults have that tells you something awful has happened.

The next thing I recall is sitting on the front steps beside Hank. He held the shotgun in both fists, barrel pointing down. You could feel heat coming off it. There were spots of blood on his work boots and the cuffs of his pants. The odour of burnt gunpowder was in the air. A faint smell of whiskey, too. Hank shifted on the steps. Then he propped his chin on the butt of the shotgun and stared over the rooftops of the houses on the other side of Spruce Road towards the mine. Only a few minutes had elapsed since Hank had come home. The sky was still mostly dark, though a dim glow came from the pits on the horizon, and there were the sounds of machinery rumbling in the distance. Somewhere in there Mr. Butler from across the street stuck his head out the front door and shouted to my mother to come get Scottie – I couldn't remember seeing him arrive.

Then Father reappeared. He had a towel in one hand. It was soaked with blood. "Hank," he said softly, "give me that now." He took the shotgun out of Hank's hands and passed it to me. "Put that in the shed," he said.

When I stood Hank said, "No." He reached for the gun.

I glanced toward the front door where Father had disappeared.

"I'm okay," Hank said. He studied the barrel for a moment. His hands shook.

I didn't know what had happened inside the house but I said, "I know."

"I'm all right now, Andy," he said. He motioned toward the gun.

He seemed to need to have something to hold onto, so I didn't argue. I laid the stock in his lap. I sat down beside him again, sensing the concrete cold through my pants. I needed to pee again. "I know," I repeated.

"You're a good fellow, Andy," Hank said. He was breathing heavily and in short gasps. "Not like –" He waved his free arm in a circle.

"I try," I said, "but my mother says I'm nothing to rave about." She had gone up the steps, my mother, and was waiting for Mr. Butler to bring Scottie out to her.

"Sure. She doesn't want you to get a swelled head is all."

"I guess."

In the silence we left I heard footsteps coming and going behind us.

"Christ," he said. "I've done something really bad." When I looked at him, his mouth was pursed and he was shaking his head from side to side. Then he cleared his throat. "Promise me something, will you, your old coach? Promise me you'll try to stay that way. The way you are now."

I didn't have a clue what he meant but I could tell it was important to him. "Sure," I said.

He smiled at me then in a grim way. "Good," he said. "That's right."

I cleared my throat but couldn't come up with anything to say.

After a while Hank said, "I'll tell you one thing, I've never been this hot in my whole life. Never." He stood the shotgun on end again, barrel pointing down, and rested his forehead against the wood stock.

By this time Mother had come out of the Petersons' house with Scottie. She paused on the top step for a moment and put her free hand on Hank's shoulder. Then she walked down the steps and stood right in front of me, with Scottie hanging on her hip. She said, "Listen real careful. I don't want you going near that bedroom. Do you understand me? Do you understand, Andrew Armin Buechler?" Ordinarily she called me *Andy,* like everyone else, but she upped the ante this way when she wanted what she said to sink in – from *Andrew* to *Andrew Armin.* This was the first time she'd used all three names. I nodded.

I did go home and get Hank a glass of water. I seemed to float between the houses. I don't recall what I was thinking. Maybe that something exciting had finally happened in Red Rock. Maybe that I was getting a drink for a murderer and that made me an accomplice. I have no memory of taking a tumbler from the cupboard or running the water, but I recall the hungry way Hank took it from me when I came back. After he finished drinking he went on saying, "I'm hot. I'm sure hot."

Other people had arrived by then, but no one else went into the house. They stood on the sidewalk, a collection of ghostly outlines becoming increasingly more distinct as light tinged the sky. Someone muttered Hank's name and then mine. Behind us Father and Mr. Butler scurried from room to room, calling out to each other. At one point I heard one of them shout *tourniquet,* and later *both legs and heave.*

I looked toward Birch Crescent where the Red Rock Works department was beginning to pave the streets. Graders and front-end loaders stood idle by the side of the road, their wheels and tires coated in red iron dust. Soon the workers with their lunches in metal boxes would be arriving and starting up the engines. Kids would be getting their books ready for school. I wondered what I was doing on Hank Peterson's steps at that moment, and if I'd be going to school with the rest of the kids in an hour or so. What was Hank feeling right then? He looked calm, feet planted wide apart on the steps. I felt my knees trembling beneath my palms. I wished Gordy McCabe was with me.

Hank stirred. He looked at me and said, "You'd think that when a man does something that out of the ordinary he'd be able to say why, wouldn't you?"

Sirens wailed in the distance. "Yes." I studied the spots of blood spattered on his boots, "I would."

"That's the funny thing. I can't." Hank shook his head. "I can't get my mind around it now. I could an hour ago when I was driving home, but now I can't seem to focus on a single thing. Not one." He sighed and shook his head, as if he was trying to clear it. He ran one hand through his hair.

We sat like that for some minutes, and I guess Hank was thinking about how his life had changed from one thing to another in less time than it takes to walk round the block. An hour ago he had been a simple thing – a grunt miner, a father, a husband – and now he was a killer, a murderer. Maybe he was thinking about what would happen next, wondering what would become of him and Scottie, where he would go, how he would put his day-to-day life back together – if he was to have one at all. I was thinking about that, thinking it for him, sort of. But I was also thinking about how ordinary everything seemed despite what had happened. Lights went off and on in neighbours' houses, children's voices floated in the air, motors started. I smelled bacon frying and something burning, leaves, maybe. Somewhere people were getting out of bed, brushing their teeth, people who would only hear about Hank and Becky after they got home from work that night. It struck me that I had not been much affected by the events myself: my heart was beating regularly and I was calm. I wondered what I would eat for breakfast that morning – pancakes and syrup maybe. I was thinking how when the worst thing you can imagine happening happens, everything goes along just the same anyway. I realized again that I was becoming an adult.

A bluejay landed in one of Hank's trees and screeched at us. "I'm cold," I said. I hadn't realized it until that moment, but I was trembling all over. The sun was almost up, the sky a mixture of pinks and greys. I hugged my arms around my body. Hank was wearing a cotton work shirt, but he was sweating through it and didn't seem to notice the cold.

"It's all so unreal is what it is," he said. "Yesterday I was worrying about having the valves re-ground on the car, whether we could afford it.... That's odd, now that I think about it, because I should have been worrying about what I'd do after the layoffs but I wasn't. You follow? There I was focused on the small stuff instead of what was really important. Maybe that's been my whole problem all along, not being able to focus on the right thing at the right time." He snorted. "And I never did get those spruces planted on the west side."

It was incoherent, but the longest speech I'd heard Hank make away from the hockey rink. "I'll get more water," I offered.

"Good," Hank said. And then he tapped the butt of the shotgun on the steps. It made a dull hollow sound, *clunk, clunk clunk,* and chipped off bits of cement.

I stood and took a few steps toward our house.

"No wait," Hank said, "don't bother." He'd been holding the tumbler in one hand, the barrel of the shotgun in the other. He looked at the tumbler as if seeing it for the first time and then dropped it into the bushes beside the steps.

I sat down again. We had all emerged from the half-light, like figures coming clear in a developing photograph. I heard a sound from the direction of our house and when I looked over there my two kid sisters were standing at my bedroom window waving. It must have seemed like a holiday to them, so many adults bustling around excited about something. Maybe school would be called off. I waved back.

"You know," Hank said, "I liked Tommy Piper. Do you believe that?"

I nodded yes I did.

"I liked him," Hank repeated. "I used to see him at the Rockland and I always liked how happy he looked. Never a care in the world. I've always been one to brood too much about things, it's a fault that Becky…but Tommy was the happy-go-lucky type. He got a big bang out of life." We sat silently after that. Hank's breathing had returned to normal. The sirens were getting close. We looked up together and saw the ambulance make the corner at Maple Avenue, its red light flashing. Hank said, "Do you understand anything I'm saying to you?"

"Yes," I said.

"You're a good boy, Andy. Never forget that."

"I think it's sad."

"Me too." He threw the shotgun where he'd thrown the water tumbler. It landed with a thud.

"What the hell," Hank said. He looked at his hands. If I hadn't known the red smears on his palms were grime from the mines I might have mistaken them for blood. Looking at them I felt edgy. I wanted Hank to go inside and wash them off, I guess.

Then the police cruiser was there, and we moved off the steps to the sidewalk, like two birds who suddenly know it's time to take flight. I was standing shoulder to shoulder with Hank and I noticed we were nearly the same height. I felt good about that. Light had come fully into the sky by then, but it was a gloomy and overcast morning. Dogs were sniffing around the trees. More neighbours, people from further down the street, had come out of their houses and were standing in a clutch on the sidewalk in front of the house, whispering together. Hank put his hand on my shoulder and then thought better of it and shoved both hands in his pockets.

Chief Dixon jumped out of the police cruiser. He and Hank played on the MineKings team that had travelled to Trail, BC, the winter before. I'd seen him with his shirt off, shovelling gravel in the Petersons' driveway with Hank. He came around the front of the car fast. "Hank," he shouted.

I felt Hank's body tense beside me. "Good-bye, Andy," he whispered.

I looked at him and then turned my eyes from his. "So long," I said.

"Think about what I asked you before."

I wanted to tell Hank I would, but Dixon started shoving Hank up the steps of the house. Things had been moving pretty slowly until then, and Hank looked bewildered by the change of pace. He shrugged one shoulder as if to brush Dixon off, but the police chief had an iron grip on Hank's arm. He told Hank to go straight into the house. He told him not to talk to anyone. He was being a cop – shouting things, pushing people around. Father and Mr. Butler had come out of the house. Dixon shouted something at them too. Then he wanted to know where the shotgun was – and when I tried to show him, he knocked me down, making sure he got to it first. The grass was wet and cold where it soaked through my trouser leg. Mr. Butler helped me to my feet. "Come on," he whispered to me through a gauze of alcohol, "Hank will be okay now." Dixon was still shouting stuff and I felt suddenly sick to the stomach. Then Father took me home. I climbed into my bed wearily. I pulled the covers up and the pillows over my head so I couldn't hear what was going on at the Petersons'.

I stayed there for two days.

Stench

Lyle Butler:

The stench.

That comes back.

I have to work at it to picture the details of Hank's face: nose, lips, all that. So much time has passed, so many faces. Could not place his voice if I heard it. But sometimes walking round the sea wall I catch a whiff of rotting fish and knots of seaweed washed up on the beach, a thick, cloying smell. Awful. *Hank Peterson.* His name pops into my head. Just like that.

I was one of the first into the bedroom. Newspapers got that part right. Almost keeled over at the smell. Roy too. Roy Buechler. He'd run into the house just before me. *Whump,* you know, *whump,* we'd heard the sound at the same time and reacted about the same way. Scared the daylights out of me. Even though I knew it was coming. Had known for weeks, for months.

Roy had Hank by the arm. I'd taken the concrete steps into the house two at a time and was standing gasping for breath in the hallway. Roy and Hank at the far end, coming out of the bedroom together like a couple of drinking buddies at the end of a binge, one helping the other. There was an overhead bulb on in the bedroom and they were cocooned in its golden light. But they were yelling at each other, too. "Move," Roy was demanding. "Not her, not my bloody wife," Hank insisted. They pulled at each other's arms.

That's when I first smelled it.

Hank's face was grey. *Ashen,* they say in the papers, but that is not right. Hard to get the colour down exact. Green, maybe, more than grey. His eyes were sunk back into the sockets. He looked sixty, sixty-five, an old man, the old man he would be one day. That is the impression, anyway.

The stench, though. Abattoir. Visited one when I was in pharmacy school, an awful exercise, do not know whose idea that was. Blood, shit, piss, sweat all mixed together. And something else. The dense and sickening odour of fear, the reek of Death.

That was what it was like in the Petersons' house that morning: and the odour of gunpowder, too. I became dizzy for a moment and put one hand on the wall to steady myself.

I heard moaning coming from the back bedroom.

Then Hank was saying, "It was not her, it was not my wife."

Roy said, "Go to the living-room, Hank. Now."

Roy looked pretty shaken. He had been with the army in Europe, but that was a long time ago. Told me about it once. Flame throwers, an Italian village up in smoke, the stench of burning flesh, women and kids. He was not proud of what he had done in the service of his country. This was different.

"It was not her," Hank repeated.

"Christ," Roy said, "get a hold of yourself, Hank." He had spotted me at the far end of the hall. "Give me that gun, now, give it to Lyle."

Hank's eyes rolled and when he looked at me, I don't think he had any idea who I was. "No," he shouted.

The soles of their shoes were covered in blood and urine and they were sliding around on the linoleum flooring.

"Give us a hand," Roy bellowed.

"All right," I shouted back, "I'm trying." I felt like vomiting. I wanted to get Hank out of there – and myself, too. We were shouting at each other, but I remember thinking Becky had it coming, little bitch.

"Hank," Roy repeated, "give Lyle the goddamn gun."

I hadn't noticed the shotgun until that moment. Hank held it, barrel pointed downward along one leg. He was trembling. There were patches of sweat the size of dinner plates under his arms. He looked at me as if I was trying to take away a toy. "No." He pressed it tighter to his body.

He was still in his miner's garb. Mud-caked boots, blue wool socks, heavy denim pants streaked red from the iron ore they dug out of the shield. I expected to see his black tin lunch bucket in one hand. The miners bought all that stuff at Fred's Hardware in the first twenty minutes after they got off the train. A uniform of sorts. Then they went down to the pits and clumped about in the work boots, wrenched the ore from the earth. It was dirty work and they were dirty men. Crude, loud-mouthed, most of them, men who could not find employment doing anything else. The union gave out they were the salt of the earth. They were not. Scum of the earth, more like.

I went down into the mine one time. Open house, that kind of thing, let the town's folk see what it's all about. They gave you a hard hat with a lamp attached to the front and took you down into the mine in an elevator. Steel flooring, wire mesh walls, the clanking and grinding of metal cables. There were signs all over the walls of the elevator: DANGER, KEEP HANDS IN, WAIT UNTIL CAR STOPS MOVING. Dark as Hades down there. Wet, smelly. The elevator car came to a lurching stop deep in the earth. Clank, crunch. Not a place for the claustrophobic. You stepped off the elevator into what seemed to be an endless black hole. Water running somewhere in the distance. Voices echoing in the tunnels.

You had to bend over at the waist and keep your head down or you'd hit the roof of the mine shaft with your skull. Crept along like that for fifty yards or more, the lamp on your hard hat splashing light on the rough walls of the tunnels. My back was sore by the time we reached the larger opening in the earth where the actual mining was going on. Don't know how the miners didn't all have wrecked backs. Understood why I sold so many packets of Dodd's Kidney Pills over the counter. Up until that visit thought it was the wives. Pregnancy and all that.

About the mine, I cannot remember much more. Miner cradling a drill in both arms like a machine gun. All his limbs vibrating when the drill bit sank into the rock. Incredible clamour. Bits of earth and rock flying around. Dust in your face. Chunks of stone falling from the roof. An awful business. In two minutes it felt as if the noises were coming from inside your own body. It was clammy down there, and close. The whole time I had the impression the roof was going to cave in on me at any moment. Wanted to get up to the fresh air again. I cannot imagine how grown men do that work in those conditions forty hours a week for fifty weeks of the year. Inhuman. Must have driven more than a few stark raving mad.

The thing about miners. Stolid eyes. Faces lined with the grime of their work. Hands too. A brutal life.

Hank's face was streaked with grime when he and Roy came up to me in the hallway. We were all in a state of panic, shouting at each other, pushing. Our blood was up. "It's dangerous," I shouted at Hank, "the gun." His shirt was filthy, smeared with hand prints as red as blood. He had not washed before he left the pits.

"Give it to me, now!" I virtually screamed in his face.

He said something to me. It was not kind. Miners never were.

After they'd passed me, Roy looked over his shoulder and signalled me to go into the bedroom. Guided Hank toward the front of the house. I could hear Hank's boots clumping over the hardwood floor and Roy continuing to talk in a low rumble.

Becky – what once had been Becky – lay on the bed. You might have thought that would have been an eyeful, Becky without clothes, but this was just a naked body lying on a mattress, legs twisted, arms crooked around the head, flung there at the moment before impact, as if trying to protect herself.

She was not entirely naked. There was the wedding ring.

One shoulder above the breasts had been ripped open and had become a mass of bloody meat. Bits of flesh stuck to the wall behind and above the bed, where a picture hung, depicting a fall scene in the woods, trees and snow. One side of Becky's head had been blown away. The ear gone.

She didn't deserve that, no one deserved that. I forced my breathing to slow. There was a grey blanket scrunched up at the foot of the bed, and I pulled it over the body as best I could without disturbing anything. As I did so, my hand touched Becky's side. Still warm.

On the far side of the room, between the bed and the wall, lay Tommy. Face to the floor. He was wearing an undershirt and boxer shorts, the shirt soaked through with blood. It looked as if he'd been hit in the back and had fallen and hadn't moved since. His shorts were stained brown and dripping urine. He was still alive. One foot twitched, scraped the floor. The sounds I had heard before had come from him. He was moaning like a baby.

That's when I thought of Scott. I stood silently by the bed, listening for crying or the bleating noises children make when they're scared. I had noticed a door along the hallway that was closed and guessed that it was his. If there is a God, I thought, He will keep young Scott sleeping for the next little while. Though how he had slept through the noise of those shots, and then our shouting, I do not know. Kids. He had just turned two. I had seen him on the sidewalk with Kelly Spelchak a day or so earlier, on a tricycle. Losing his balance and tumbling off in the heedless way of toddlers, but getting right back on the seat again as soon as Kelly had picked him up and brushed him off. When he was teething a few months ago, I had prescribed him a mild pain killer. *For Scott Peterson* I'd typed in tiny black letters on the label. I was relieved there was no crying coming from his room.

I bent over Tommy's body and pressed a finger against his jugular. The stench coming off him took my breath away. Faint pulse though. A pool of blood under him and more oozing from his arm. It needed to be staunched. I thought *police, ambulance.* I had seen a phone on a table in the hallway, and as I skirted the bed to reach it I tried to remember the number of the hospital. Near the doorway blood and urine streamed across the floor. Whoever came into the room next was sure to slip in it. We needed to clean that up. Needed towels and washcloths, too, to sop up the yellow pool around Tommy's body.

After making two phone calls I took off my tie and stuffed it into my jacket pocket. Lyle Butler would not be filling prescriptions for a few hours.

From the hall I called out to Roy to make a tourniquet for Tommy. He answered *what?* and I shouted back louder than I'd intended: *tourniquet.*

By then Hank had gone out onto the front step and was sitting with Roy's son, Andy. They were friends of sorts, I recalled, a little-leaguer and his coach, a boy and his hero. Hank's chin rested on his hands, which he'd crossed on the butt of the shotgun, shoulders slumped forward. From the back he looked completely done in. I wished I could give him something to help him through the next few hours. I was afraid for him and afraid for Andy, too, the gun being so close at hand, but Roy said it was all right, that Hank was calm now, and in any case, there were no shells in the chambers. Roy had checked.

I glanced out the front window. We had done what we could for Tommy Piper, stopped the bleeding, cleaned his legs, covered him with warm blankets. We were working with the towels on the floor while waiting for the ambulance and the deplorable Dixon. Roy's breath came in short, rasping gasps. At one point he put his head down and retched. I went and fetched him a glass of water. After that I called for Helen Buechler to collect young Scott, and she came in pale and shivery and took him away, wrapped in a blue quilt I found in his closet.

It was then that I noticed the crowd gathering out front. Light had come into the sky, with a pink tint to it, and my neighbours had transformed from outlines to three-dimensional figures.

Later I heard that people thought we had done the wrong thing, Roy and me, by cleaning up before Dixon and the ambulance boys arrived. *Meddling,* someone called it. Probably an idea they got from some of the lawyers that flocked to Red Rock in the days right after the shootings. Disturbing the evidence. What nonsense. You don't stand idly by when another human is bleeding to death, even if the person is Tommy Piper. Even if you do end up with urine and blood and shit all over your trousers and hands. You do what you can. People who say things like that are fools. Frightened by life – of consequences – but guilty about their cowardice, too, so they point the accusing finger at anyone who isn't shit scared of life, hoping to shift the spotlight from their own pathetic characters.

I was hoping Jonathan was not one of them.

He had been sore at me for a stretch of time.

I had seen him the night before and he had told me he was moving in the spring, *definitely moving,* he'd said. I'd heard – at least every month going on for two years – how he was leaving Red Rock once and for all, but this time he shot a new line at me.

"You too, Lyle," he said.

"Me?"

"Right," he said. "It's time to pull up stakes. You always say a person has to know when it's time to move – and now's the time."

"You must be kidding."

"No."

"Good lord. Why?"

Jonathan was sitting on the couch facing the TV, and I had to turn in my chair to face him. "You know why."

I was drinking brandy and took a good swig. "I know I complain a lot. About the hypocrisy of Red Rock and what not. But is it that easy? You just light out?"

"It's that simple. Nothing is ever easy."

"You mean for us?"

"I mean for anybody. But now you mention it, for the likes of us, yes. I mean – these hypocrites are all over us here."

"I don't know," I said. "Starting up all over again."

"You're just a joke around here," Jonathan said, po-faced. "A bad joke at that." He was drinking Red Cap ale from the bottle, and to emphasize his point he banged it down on the Duncan Phyfe table between us. My prize possession, and he knew it.

I stifled a grimace and took a swig of brandy. In his last year of high school Jonathan's father had called him a fairy, among other things, and thrown him out of the house and he had been living in 4F since. That's how we'd come to know each other. What made things between us so convenient, being in the same building and all, one floor apart, no complicated comings and goings for Red Rock's gossips to prattle about. "I thought you were proud of who you are."

"God," he said, "that's not the point."

"Oh, listen to you. What is the point – in your humble opinion?"

"The point is, towns like this eat people like us alive, Lyle. Eat us alive. You can't hide here."

It was true. I had come to Red Rock to escape, it was clear to me then but had not been at the time. I had been looking to go underground in my own way, and a town in the back woods had seemed a good place to start afresh. After Jerry's suicide, after that dreadful funeral and his family.

I still had Jerry's ring. Wore it on my pinkie. Still do.

I said weakly, "You can't *hide* anywhere."

"But you can survive. In a place like Vancouver you can live without having to put up with all this – this dissimulation. This shit."

"So we just get out, is that it? Good-bye Red Rock?"

"Why not?"

I realized my brandy snifter was empty and I got up and poured another. "Sounds like cowardice," I said.

"Survival," Jonathan said. "Anyway, isn't that your favourite topic – the way you just up and left Toronto for Red Rock after Jerry died?"

"Oh, Lord," I said, "don't remind me. That was a long time ago."

I had said it sharply and we both left a silence. Jonathan was probably wondering why he had become involved with me in the first place, or something equally dark.

I was thinking again about what Jerry's suicide and sad little funeral had taught me: that we are each and every one of us alone in this world, despite all the things we do, all the things we tell ourselves to the contrary – like building up relationships with lovers, relatives, friends, neighbours, and so on. Those entanglements we like to tell ourselves weave a safety net under us, but which have no more substance than a spider's web when you actually stumble and fall one day.

Oddly enough, the idea did not frighten me, the idea that what you can expect from other people is nothing. You might, from time to time – like the proverbial bolt out of the blue – be the recipient of generosity or support, sometimes of the breath-taking variety – people will surprise you with goodness. But you should not expect it. What you should expect is double-dealing, an infinite variety of betrayals, and most often nothing at all. Which is pretty darn upsetting. Realizing that to everyone else you are nothing more than a cipher. Nobody gives a damn about what's going on in your life, is what it amounts to. They might smile or mutter some words, comforting words, even, but you're on your own, and that's that. You have to face the travails of life alone and deal with them.

Dark thoughts.

"That was a long time ago," I repeated to Jonathan. "Another country."

Jonathan has a Roman nose, and his nostrils flare when he's angry. "Listen to you," he said. *"A long time ago…starting all over…."*

"You don't realize, Jon, what it takes to establish yourself in business, to build a reputation, to make –"

"You're afraid."

"If you think so, Jon."

He sighed. "You're a coward is what it amounts to. An old man."

It was the kind of conversation we'd been having more often lately, and for a moment I loathed Jonathan. What could he know about what it takes to have the rug pulled out from under you when you came home and looked in the bathroom one night? He was a nice boy, but only a boy when all was said and done. Besides, he had that temper and was so filled with rage he was a danger to himself and anyone near him, me especially. The old fag.

That's what Hank had said to me in the hallway. *Fag.* So unoriginal, so sad, in a way. Like what he had done. But I forgave him for saying it. Even though it hurt.

When the ambulance arrived I was at the bathroom sink, wringing blood and urine out of towels. The stench was overpowering. I had had some water to drink and splashed my face too. Nausea, though.

Dizziness. You do not wash away what we saw in there.

The house had become quiet, eerily so. It seemed like the past twenty minutes had occurred in a dream. I had to force my mind away from Becky's body and on to what was right in front of me: the soaked and stinking towels, my shirt with patches of blood on it, my stained hands. Days later I was still scrubbing at red stains under my nails.

In the bathroom mirror I saw that my face was flushed and hair matted to my forehead with sweat. We had been working hard.

Outside a crowd had grown.

People stood in groups, whispering and nodding. Most still dressed in housecoats and slippers, shivering with cold as they tried to assess how this disaster would affect their own lives. Believing that it wouldn't. Jonathan was standing alone on the sidewalk, his hair screwed in a knot from sleeping. The dishevelment was charming. I wanted to go to him, to hold him, but I stood in the freezing air next to Roy Buechler and tried not to think of that.

Roy and I had been thrown together by fate, being the first to arrive at the scene. Though we had never so much as shared a cup of coffee before, we were linked perhaps forever, in our own thoughts and in the minds of the townspeople with Hank and Becky and Tommy and their gory drama. That's the way it is with disasters. I cannot think of that morning without sensing Roy at my side, without hearing his breathing just before he retched, without sensing his eyes shift from the sky to the house to Hank, and then back to the sky.

Wisps of smoke rose from the chimneys of our neighbours' houses and curled when the breeze above ground level tugged at them. It had been mostly dark when Roy and I had run into the Petersons' house, but now a thin light spread from horizon to horizon. Grey clouds hung over the valley, the kind that form at the start of day, then never move. Everything seemed washed-out, lacking outline. Houses a block or so down from the Petersons' were pale and ghostly, as if on the far side of a smoked-glass window. In the distance the pines on the big hill were a greenish mass that faded into background.

Our breath made ghosts over our heads. It felt like it might snow.

The ambulance had pulled up near Hank's car. By that time he had come off of the front step and was standing on the grass with Andy Buechler, looking as if he, too, were only a spectator, as if when the ambulance left, he would be able to walk away from the bodies and blood with the rest of us and sit down to a strong cup of coffee. He rubbed his nose from time to time and looked about. The shotgun had disappeared.

While we stood watching the attendants remove the stretchers from the ambulance, Roy's younger girl trotted up with a jacket for each of us.

Roy asked me, "Did you get all the cloths?"

"Yes," I said.

"The ones under the bed?"

"They were putrid."

"I had forgotten… that people's bowels…."

"I put them in the bathroom sink. With the towels."

"Tommy's clothes?"

"On a pile with hers. Near the door."

"The shell casings were there."

"I left them," I said, "for Dixon."

"That's right," he said.

"Uh-huh."

"And Hank seems okay?"

"He's calm now. Thank God."

"You?"

"Better, thanks. That was like nothing I'd ever seen."

"Or want to again."

"You can count on that."

"It's the little guy I feel sorry for."

"Yes. Poor Scott. No child should have to go through this."

"No child, for sure, and no living person."

"You're right there. Not even Tommy."

We smiled grimly at each other. There seemed little else to say. I was thinking the future for little Scott seemed dim. It looked as if his grandparents, Sam and Christine Johnson, would be raising him, and that would be terrible for the kid. Mother dead, father in jail. How could a child grow up without either parent? And what were the Johnsons likely to tell him about what had happened? They would take sides, and yet a son should not be raised hearing his father killed his mother. Things are difficult enough between fathers and sons. Maybe the Johnsons would take the kid away or try to stop Hank from visiting him. That would be ugly as well as illegal, probably. I knew

Christine Johnson had a heart condition. All this kerfluffle might bring on the coronary her medication was supposed to fend off. But Sam Johnson would never stand for Scott being raised by strangers.

It was a mess for sure.

I have never believed in raising children away from their parents – private schools and the like – as I have always believed that the way kids behave is a direct reflection of their mothers and fathers. It all starts at home. And I've regretted, yes, that I will never have children of my own. When I see babies in the store, hanging on to their mothers, their little faces shining, their hands grabbing at everything on the shelves, I think it's a shitty world when the only thing that counts when it comes to kids is biology. Anyone who pairs up with a woman can have a carload full, whether or not they have an ounce of love in their veins. And a lot don't. I see it from the other side of the counter, when the mothers come in for ointments and drugs to treat the bruises and malnourishment they inflict on their own flesh and blood. Just thinking about it, my mind goes blank.

There are worse things done every day in towns like Red Rock than squeezing the trigger of a shotgun.

Shortly after, Dixon pulled up in the police cruiser, the siren shrieking.

He must have another name, Dixon, but that's all

anyone ever calls him. He's a burly man with thick dark hair and a swagger that stretches from the Red Rock police station clear across the Great Lakes. A real brute. He had fought in the Korean War, his major qualification for the job of Police Chief – his only qualification, having machine-gunned some fellow humans and grown callous in a dug-out in some freezing place in Asia. He was no hero. Certainly had no touch with people. He leapt from the cruiser and slammed the car door behind him, all in one motion, letting us know that he was the man in charge.

"Hank," he said curtly.

Hank gave him that blank stare. "Dixon," he said. "Dixon, I –"

"Hank," Dixon repeated, "you come with me now."

"I started the engine, I drove here from the pits...." Hank was holding his hands out front, clenching and unclenching his fists.

"Come on, Hank," Dixon said, reaching one arm out.

"The shotgun, I didn't want to give it up but –"

"Talk sense now, Hank. Just talk sense." Dixon's hand on Hank's arm spun him around so they both faced the house.

Andy Buechler was standing next to Hank.

"Don't you see," the kid said, "he's not thinking right yet."

"You," Dixon said to Andy, "you get on home now."

"But –"

"Now. Home."

"It's okay," Roy said, stepping to the boy's side, "he and Hank –"

"This is no place for kids. You hear? Or meddling adults."

Andy took a step back. He was about to protest when Roy said, "Don't worry, son, Hank's okay now, aren't you, Hank?"

Hank opened his mouth to speak but Dixon shoved his shoulder, pushing him toward the steps. Dixon wheeled on the crowd. "No place for any of you," he shouted. He waved his hand in the air and raised his voice. "Go on home, now, the lot of you." He stood with his feet wide apart, waiting. When people started to shuffle about, he turned to Hank and asked, "Where's the gun?"

Hank said, "It wasn't her. Not Becky."

Dixon stepped forward and put his face up to Hank's, real close. They were both short men with big heads. Dixon was wearing his cop's cap and the bill was no more than an inch from Hank's forehead. He said, "I want the gun."

"Can't you see," I said, "that he's in no state for this – for questioning."

Dixon turned. "If I want your help," he said, "I'll sing out for it."

"I just –"

"Real loud." He glanced at me and almost said the words going through his little boy's brain. I was waiting for them, but Andy interrupted.

"In the bushes there," Andy offered. "The rose bushes."

The boy took a step in that direction, but Dixon

threw out his arm and yanked him back by the collar. The boy fell to his knees.

"I'll take care of it," Dixon said. "You get on home." He stepped away from Hank to where the gun had fallen, lifted it out of the bushes, and in a moment was back at Hank's side.

My heart was racing. Blood surged in my neck. I was at Andy's side, helping him to his feet. "Come on now," I whispered. "Hank will be all right."

"Yes," Roy said. "That's right."

"*All* of you," Dixon said, "get on home." He had hold of Hank's arm, the shotgun gripped in his other hand. "This is a police matter. Official business." He fixed us with a glare. "If I need statements, I know where to find you." He waved his hand in the air again. "So push off. Now."

"C'mon," Roy said. He motioned with his head to Andy and they set off across the grass together, Roy with his hand on his son's back. I had given them back the jacket. I was shivering with cold. When they were on their own lawn he turned to me and asked, "You okay?"

"I'm all right. It's just –"

"Yeah," he said.

"It's just that Dixon is such a mug...."

"I know. Our representative of justice."

"Those aren't the words I was thinking."

"I know." We both snorted and cut our eyes in Dixon's direction.

Roy's hair was matted to his forehead, too. He seemed older than his forty or so years. Tired. He shrugged. "What the heck," he said.

"You're right," I said, "what the hell." I stood watching for a moment longer, until Dixon and Hank disappeared into the Petersons' house. I cursed Dixon under my breath and vowed to be a pain in the ass when he came round with his questions. Arrogant mug.

I looked for Jonathan and when I saw that he'd already gone back to his place, I decided to take a walk around the block to clear my head. Something he'd said was rattling round in my dull brain. I wanted a drink bad, but I knew it would set my heart pounding in my chest. No point bringing on a coronary. When you're under stress you have to learn to slow down. Anyway, there would be time enough for that later, drinking. I had already made up my mind to stay home for the rest of day. Had to think through what I had seen before I reached for the sherry.

I can tell you it helped.

In those days I drank sherry mixed with orange juice. Drank a lot of it. Especially when I sat in the leather chair for a good think, which I did for a few nights after the death of Becky, TV on for background noise. Thinking about Hank and Becky and Tommy.

I had been watching them caught in the old three-way tug-of-war for a year, and I feared the worst, especially for Hank. Tommy was a survivor. And

Becky would land on her feet. Becky the Cat, I'd heard someone call her.

When she came into the store you could tell she was used to being the centre of attention. I knew from the swift click of high heels on the floor tiles that she had come through the front door, and I always glanced up to see her black curls bobbing along the aisles. She was an attractive woman in lots of ways. Physically, of course. Breasts, a nice ass. Skin like alabaster. But she was filled with tremendous life energy, too. I've always been a sucker for that. Though with Becky that vibrancy had got twisted inside her somehow.

She was one of those women who aren't happy married. Restless and unhappy, always fighting something, her own demons, you might say. It didn't make her any less attractive, maybe more, giving her a nervous energy that you were tempted to think you might be able to tame and make your own. There are people like that, devilishly irresistible, and they are almost always bad for the ones who fall under their spell.

She was trouble. Not an awful person. Just frivolous and superficial. Hank had landed himself a handful there.

It was not difficult to understand what he saw in her. She exuded sex: the tight skirts and sweaters she wore, her perfume. Even the way she said *damn* when she dug in her purse for change. Made my flesh creep.

When Becky came into the store the eyes of every man followed her up and down the aisles. She was the sexiest woman in town, though there may have been others prettier. It was the way she walked. In her high heels she tipped forward with each step, looking as if she was on the verge of losing her balance and was about to fall flat on her face, and something in you wanted to rush down the aisle and grab her up in your arms before that happened. The idea must have haunted many men's fantasies. I never actually saw that occur, but I did see men leaning forward as if they were about to make the dash to her side – and I had to keep from laughing aloud.

In any case, Becky was too big a handful for Hank, who once you got past the chiselled good looks was really a simple fellow who liked sports and puttering in the yard and wanted no more to complete his fantasy world than two kids in strollers and a Chevy in the front drive. Hank the Home Body. But the good looks were enough for Becky Johnson when she met Hank, just out of high school and chafing against Red Rock and her parents. She threw herself at him, hoping, without knowing it, probably, that he would rescue her. And when a *Playboy* bunny type does that an ordinary guy is doomed, even if he suspects there's something amiss in what's happening to him. He has so little to fall back on, no way of knowing the girl's not in love with *who* he is but *what*.

Then, too, it's hard for a man like Hank not to believe he isn't the answer to every girl's dreams – or that he might be making a mistake in loving a woman who's too good-looking for him.

That's a possibility few men give any thought to.

In matters of the heart a man is best off with a woman who's afraid, just a smidge, that she might lose him to someone else. Otherwise he must be shameless in his devotion – or he will lose *her*. This is what Hank Peterson did not understand, though he had married a dame who was so sexy she must have known by the time she was sixteen that she could have any man in Red Rock for the asking.

She should have known it by eighteen. That would have saved a lot of grief. Hank was blind to that. Happy to coach kids and trundle wheelbarrows of dirt around his yard and make love to Becky 2.3 times a week, content in the knowledge that her love was secure because he had swept a little high school nymph off her feet fresh out of gym class, before she had had an orgasm or learned to smoke a cigarette properly. Dumb.

Tommy Piper was no better.

They'd probably been carrying on for months before anyone noticed, before I did, though I have a nose for deceit that comes from practicing it so long. But when I did catch on, my heart sank. Yes, actually sank. It was a ridiculous moment, and when I remember it I have to chuckle despite what's happened since. I was at the back of the store one day mixing compounds when Tommy came up and asked for condoms, not the way most men do, blushing, whispering, the ones that don't send their wives to buy them, but in his normal voice, the way he would have asked for aspirin. While I was busy at the counter finding the brand he wanted, Becky came into the store – I heard her high heels – and both Tommy and I swivelled our heads toward the door. When he was finished looking, he turned back to me with a lizard smirk, and though I've never liked Tommy and his loud-mouth crowd, I remember thinking he had a right to ogle Becky. By this time I'd passed a dozen condoms to Tommy and he was heading down the aisle to the cashier. Ordinarily I would have turned back to my work and missed what happened next, but because it was Becky walking toward me I lingered at the counter an extra moment or so, just to get my own eye full. When she and Tommy passed he made a motion with the package in his hand, like tinkling a bell, and they both ducked their heads the tiniest bit and Becky giggled, the way teenagers do, and put one hand over her mouth.

The meaning of that giggle was clear to me. I dropped the prescription bottle I was holding and it smashed on the floor into a hundred pieces. I saw it all coming: the secret meetings, the gossiping, the shotgun, the blood.

Not that I imagined those exact details. I can't claim that. But I knew from the kinds of people Hank and Becky were what sequence of events was bound to unfold before too long. Becky had this urge, she had to carry on, the bitch. And Hank was not used to dealing with his emotions, and that meant he would not confront Becky when he found out she had been slutting around, so there would be no second chance for them. No talking it out or resolving things in a civilized way. Something violent had to happen.

It made me sick to think about it and sicker to know there was nothing I could do to prevent it, an aging fairy, the butt of God knows how many jokes. Who wanted my advice?

But there were many mornings that summer and fall when I stood at the bay window of my apartment in the early light of day, festering. I saw Tommy's car parked behind the rink. Once or twice I saw Tommy himself, ducking out the back door of the Petersons' house, then scurrying to his car. Hardly more than a shadow, the studs on his black leather jacket glinting light as he flitted below the street lamps newly installed by the town. Sometimes a light would go on in the house afterwards, Becky in the kitchen before returning to the bed she and Tommy had made warm. I wondered if she ever thought about Hank or young Scott. Probably not.

Those mornings when he left the Petersons', Tommy always glanced around before getting in the car. And he never turned on the head lamps until he had backed down the gravel drive beside the rink and was on to Maple Avenue. Then he drove toward the mine road before doubling back to the centre of town and his apartment.

He was hopeless and dumb but also cunning. You can be both.

Hank was just blind and jealous. Oh yes, the green-eyed monster.

When he got wind of what was going on, things developed a logic of their own and there was nothing

anyone could do to stop him from pulling the trigger.
I thought that then. Think it now.

Jonathan said, "You're not leaving?" This was a night or two after Hank shot Becky and Tommy, the Sunday or Monday following, maybe.

"I'm staying put."

"You're nuts."

"I want to see what happens."

We were sitting in the leather chairs opposite each other. Brandy for me, a beer for him. It was past nine o'clock. A safe time for us.

"It's obvious what will happen. They'll string Hank up."

"They don't do that anymore."

"Gas chamber, whatever."

"Just because he's a miner, a labourer, a boy from the working class?"

Jonathan sighed. "Because he's guilty."

"You know that?"

"Everybody knows that."

I sipped from my snifter. "I want to see it through. I don't want to just run away and hide."

"That's a good one. You."

"Everyone else is behaving so shamefully. What with the reporters, a chance to get their mug on TV. I do not want to be part of that."

Jonathan rolled his eyes. "Get out," he said, "while the getting is good."

"I want to behave honourably. For once."

Jonathan rolled his eyes again and took a long swallow of beer. "They will be all over you," he said, "the reporters."

"I know."

"They will find out about you. Us."

"I know that too."

"They want to crucify someone. They'll crucify you."

"I can handle it."

"You're a fruitcake, a regular fruitcake."

"Especially if you are not here."

"Oh, I get it, you want to give me the heave-ho. Christ almighty."

"You just said it. That you're leaving."

"You're damn right about that."

We sat in silence while he finished his beer. I looked into my snifter. Our eyes did not meet. He put the empty beer bottle down on the end table near his elbow.

"It's the best for you," I managed.

"Yeah," he whispered, "I can see that."

"It is," I said. I took a swig of brandy. "It is," I repeated, "the best."

"Yeah, sure."

"In a couple months, a year, I will go, too."

Jonathan snorted. "And what's that supposed to do – make me all warm and fuzzy inside?"

"If you're in Vancouver," I said, "I will join you."

He laughed. "What's left of you."

"I will be okay," I said.

He had stood and moved to the door. "So what, I

write you, is that it, is that the sop you're throwing me, steamy letters at two thousand miles?"

"And you will too," I said, "be all right."

"Wise up," he said. He sighed and then he added as an afterthought, "But good luck with the sharks, the lawyers, the reporters."

It was just after ten o'clock that same night when the knock came. I put the snifter of brandy on the side table and went to the door.

"Mr. Butler," the man standing there said. "Or is it Doctor?" He was tall, with sensitive brown eyes that peered at you from behind tortoise shell specs.

"It's mister," I said.

"I'm –"

"A reporter," I said. "Look, I've talked to the lawyers, I've even tried talking to some of you people, but…."

"Manson Welch," he said, "*Weekend* magazine." He offered his hand, a paw that was large and gripped mine firmly but briefly. The smell of cigarette smoke came off his clothes like a vile scent. "Roy Buechler said it was you that saved Tommy Piper's life."

I had to smile at that. He smiled, too. He was wearing a mackintosh and had his hands crossed out front like an expectant child.

"That's a charming fib," I said, "but I won't help you all the same."

"You were fond of Hank, though," he said. "I've heard that. Maybe you can help him." He dropped his eyes, afraid that I would bring the interview to an end, and when I didn't he added, "I've only got two questions – three. I'll be gone in moments."

"You want," I said, "to crucify Hank, drag his name through the mud."

"I want to explain Hank, not destroy him. Truly. To explain how any man – any woman – can do something dreadful on impulse but still be the same as you or me." He patted his coat pocket, a nervous habit of chain-smokers, and said, "Five minutes."

I could see I had him on the defensive. "I won't say a bad word about Hank," I insisted. "Understand that. And I will not discuss anything medical."

"No. Good. If I want that, I can talk to their doctor."

"McCabe," I said. "Dr. Thomas McCabe."

We were standing at the door and when I backed up we crossed into the living-room. The top buttons of his mackintosh were loose and underneath he wore a teal blue sport coat and a starched white shirt with the tie off the collar. In my slacks and turtleneck I felt at a disadvantage. He took in the room, his eyes hardly pausing over the side table.

"About Hank," he said, coming directly to the point. "What state of mind was he in when you saw him that morning?"

"State of mind," I mused. "That's a good question."

"Angry? Depressed?"

"His eyes were rolling, and he was trembling, I think."

"Was he dressed as usual?"

"Work boots, a khaki shirt. Some of the miners change and shower before leaving the mines, but many come straight home from the pits." I was trying to be matter-of-fact. I sensed he liked that.

"So nothing unusual?"

"There were sweat stains under his armpits. He scared me, I have to tell you. I've never seen anyone like that and hope never to again."

"No, I would guess not. Did he say anything?"

"Some incoherent stuff. He said it wasn't Becky in there." I waved one hand in the air. "He was not himself. But he loved her. That I can tell you."

"That's Roy's reading too. Mr. Buechler."

I was expecting him to be pushy and was surprised by his deference – Mr. Butler this, Mr. Buechler that. Maybe I was wrong about him. "Hank was just another person, out of control, like," I said. "I've been turning it over in mind since and don't know quite how to put it. He was –"

"Go on."

"The word that keeps coming to me is… *dis* – …."

"Disconnected?"

"Disgusted. Like he was sick to the stomach at what he'd seen."

"He was sick to the stomach?"

"But now that you put it that way, yes, disconnected. I didn't realize it then, but I have since. In your line of work you know how ordinary lives come apart at the seams, but I don't. But that's what happens, isn't it? We go along thinking we've got things nicely under control, when really we're just holding it together with, like threads, and then something happens to us and everything unravels. That was Hank. He unravelled. Personally. Becky had done this stupid thing – slutting around – but it could have been something else, telling off the boss, crashing the car – then everyone else had to live with what she had done. The consequences. Because Becky's sleeping around sucked everyone else down with her. The people she cared about most. Think of young Scott."

We were standing in the centre of the room and I was staring at my stuff, my special objects, pictures, furniture, liquor. I don't know what made me make that speech. "Look," I said, "this is tiring me out. I'm not making sense, I am...."

"One more point," he said. I could tell by the way he fidgeted around that Manson Welch needed a cigarette as badly as I needed a brandy. But neither of us were giving in. "Where did you first see him that morning?"

"Where? Inside the house. In the hallway."

"Not *in* the bedroom?"

"By the time I got there, Roy was leading him down the hallway."

"So you didn't see the actual...."

"No, we had to run into the house. It was minutes elapsed."

"Good," he said. "Good." He patted his pockets again and I thought he was going to ask me if I minded if he lit up, when he looked at me sharply. I realized at that moment that there was more on his mind than he was letting on.

Suddenly he stepped toward me with both hands trembling. He asked, "Then where was the gun?"

"Hank had it. Roy asked him to give it me but he wouldn't. He wouldn't give it up and I guess Roy and I thought it better not to antagonize him."

"Right," he said. He ran one finger up and down his temple. "What I mean is, did you hear the shots? Earlier that morning?"

"I was shaving." I nodded in the direction of the bathroom. "In there."

"And?"

"I heard shots."

"You did? Clearly?"

"Yes. One and then another."

"Yes, that's what I understand. Not just one shot, though, or three?"

"No, no. Two. One and then the other."

"Yes." He paused. "Would you say there was a delay between them?"

I had not thought about it, and I hesitated, trying to recall the sequence of events I had believed, until that moment, I knew as well as every item in my apartment. I looked around at my books, my paintings, my plants, everything in its accustomed place, and I wished I could fix those shots as clearly. "It seemed one shot came right after the other, but now you ask, there might have been a delay. I can't say for certain."

He pursed his lips as if trying to decide whether or not to ask another question. There was a mole to the left of his mouth, a mole with a long black hair sticking from it. What he asked took me by surprise. "Would you mind if I lit a cigarette?"

"No," I said. I felt ridiculous. "I'll get an ashtray."

"That won't be necessary," he said. "I'm on my way out the door this very minute. I'm done," he said. "Finito." He took a pack of Luckies out of an inside pocket of his jacket and produced some matches from another. "What I mean is I just realized that I'm dog tired," he added. He lit up, blew smoke into the air, and then returned the cigarettes to his pocket. "Thanks for your time," he said. He straightened his coat and then shook my hand again.

I was baffled at his sudden decision to leave. "You can't realize," I said, "what this is doing to our town. Tearing it apart."

"I know," he said. "It's a dark period for your town."

"Neighbours ratting on neighbours, friends on friends. These are not really sophisticated people. But they are people who can be thoughtless. Who can turn on you."

He took a long drag. "They'll be all right," he said. "You've descended into the darkness, and if I may be pompous for a moment, your community will emerge from the darkness into the light."

"They're people who can turn on anyone. They can be cruel – and ugly."

"Things work out."

"Maybe."

"For Hank too."

"Perhaps," I said. "I don't think so."

"Things have a way," he said. "You'll see."

I had no idea what he meant, but as I closed the door behind him I realized saying the words to him had made me face the truth about Red Rock.

I was leaving.

I had to leave.

Jonathan was right. It was all just dreaming and lies. Thinking anything could ever work out now.

I strode over to the side table and poured a large brandy.

On the news there was an item about refugees from Hungary. It began with some old clips from 1956, tanks lumbering through streets and people running in panic. Most of the footage showed gaunt faces, the faces of people who had abandoned their homes and their lives and been forced to start again in new surroundings. I felt ill. But I kept watching. There was something familiar about the faces, and as I leaned close to the TV I saw what made them familiar was they had the same look as Hank's after the shootings, pale and anxious, and I thought, yes, Hank Peterson has become a refugee, only not from a country, but from the rest of mankind. He was on the outside now, too, looking in.

Like the refugees, too, Hank looked defeated. He'd killed someone and a part of himself had died, so he would never be comfortable in society again. An image flicked through my mind then: Hank sitting down to tea with the parents of one of Scott's school chums some afternoon. It would be nothing but a sham – on both sides. I knew that he was in a jail somewhere, but that it would never matter again to Hank whether he was in or out of jail, because the real sentence he had to suffer had nothing to do with courts and judges, or bricks and mortar. I knew because I'd seen that look in mirrors staring back at me.

I saw, too the course plotted out for me. Not a happy picture.

No.

I finished my brandy. I shut off the TV. After a while I got up and went into the bathroom and stood in front of the mirror. My hair was thinning on top. I picked up the water tumbler on the sink ledge, raised it, and smashed it into the glass. At first it didn't break, it just cracked, so I smashed the tumbler into it a second and then a third time, shattering my own image into thousands of jagged pieces.

Crazy Eights

Madge Cirini:

So, sure, I was there the morning they brought Tommy Piper into the Red Rock General on the stretcher, and it was not a pretty sight, let me tell you, because once you got past the smell, there was the blood, and that's the one thing you never get used to, the blood, no matter how many years you've been in the nursing game.

It was the mines, wasn't it? The men were always getting hurt. There was a steady stream of ambulances from the pits to the Emergency in the days I worked there. The conveyor belt accidents were the worst but every aspect of mining was responsible for its share of injuries. The miners doing the drilling dropped the drill parts on their feet all the time, I don't know it must have been dark down in those pits and wet, so the cold metal slipped in their hands, but even though they wore those steel-toed boots they were always coming in with crushed toes and mangled ankles. There's more than a hundred bones in the human foot and some of those young buggers managed to smash up each and every one of them, bless their clumsy souls, before they were shaving proper. The boys doing the blasting were another thing because the trick there is not to make mistakes in timing, setting off charges before the area has been given the all clear, but that's a lot to ask of dozy twenty-year-olds dreaming of beer and girls and the Lord himself only knows what else. Those were leg wounds, mostly, from flying rock and debris, though occasionally someone got it in the back or the head – the miners, especially the young ones were not always particular about wearing their hard hats, which was company policy, and union, too, but what did that ever matter. Ah, well. They were tough boys until one of their ears was cut in half or they were blinded by a projectile of sharp granite. Oh Lord. Then there were tears and the sweating like they'd pissed their pants and the passing out. The boys who did the pick and ax work, the geologists, had to scale the rock faces in the open pits and those rock faces were slippery, too, there were many falls and many broken arms and legs, not to mention backs wrenched permanently and traumatized organs. The conveyor belts were the worst.

All those whirling wheels and pulleys and cogs and teeth, they got hold of the men's clothes and just ripped off an arm or a leg, the way girls do with their dolls sometimes, only these were flesh and blood human beings that were dismembered, for sure. The ambulance brought them in along with their bleeding stumps, I don't know what we were supposed to do with those, they ended up in the garbage with the soiled and bloody clothes. Some of those poor young buggers looked like they'd been hit by a cannon ball or something, flesh and bone all chewed up and blood gushing out everywhere. It took your breath away some days. Even the guys driving the trucks: smashed fingers, wrenched knees, broken wrists, lacerations, lumps, bruises. There was a first aid station out at the pits so we didn't even see the small stuff, but we saw plenty. It was a war zone out there some days – and that wasn't counting the car accidents going to and from the graveyard shift or the fist fights or the suicides or the murders.

But I'm getting ahead of myself.

So, yes, we were in school together, Becky Johnson and me, Becky the Bombshell, we called her in those days. We got our first crinolines at the same time, Becky's pink, mine powder blue, and Ann-Marie Lundblau's mauve, oh we were a sight prancing about like princesses going to the ball, the three of us, little Red Rock queens, only one of us being truly of the blood. That was in elementary school. In Grade Twelve we wore white lipstick, and later when Becky and I went to work at the hospital we used rat tail combs to tease up each other's hair in the staff room, making bouffes on top of our heads that even we had to laugh at. What a sight! I have pictures somewhere. One of the two of us at the hospital, holding the Easter basket we made up and raffled off to raise money for the poor kids of Red Rock. We look so young. One of Becky and me and the Standish twins leaning against Arnie's car, an orange beetle that Arnie crashed into Dead Man's Curve two summers after graduating from high school, killing himself and Benny Cox. The young are in such a hurry to die. In another snap we're in someone's basement, sixteen-year-olds wearing nothing but panties and bras and feeling very self-conscious, mugging for the camera, but half ashamed of our breasts and worrying before the shutter even clicked just whose hands those photos might fall into. That would have been the night of the pajama party, when Gina Gasparini and Becky Johnson sneaked out to meet a couple of guys and went skinny dipping at Crystal Lake, or so they claimed. In that snapshot Becky's smiling the way my Trish smiles, a dimple at both corners of her mouth, and that is unsettling, your own child's face reminding you of a girlfriend of thirty years ago, but maybe the good Lord meant it that way, ensuring that I would not let my own flesh and blood slip away on me the way Becky did.

Only, Sweet Jesus, don't let history repeat itself.

We weren't such good friends, now. Becky was the centre of attention, the good-looking one, the one the boys flirted with while I hung back and smiled a lot and laughed, too loud probably, at the boys' jokes. I was a little jealous, yes, but I basked in her sunshine, too. She was slim and wore makeup and smoked cigarettes just like the guys, Luckies, someone brought them over from the States. I was gangly. My hair was naturally curly, a tangle over my ears, and I had two moles on my chin which Mother said were beauty marks, Trish has one, too, but I would have traded anything for Becky's pale white skin and bright green eyes, not to mention her slim waist and high little breasts. The eyes of all the boys used to follow her when we walked down the halls at school – teachers, too. She said to me, she said, "If you got it, Madge, baby, flaunt it," a good motto for her short life, bless her soul.

She loved parties. I've never known anyone to

dance like she did: on the gym floor, in people's basements, on the street, in the sand at the beach when we drove out to Crystal Lake and turned up the car radios. Becky kicked off her shoes, she pirouetted. While the rest of us slow waltzed, a lame excuse for necking in actual fact, she sashayed up and down the beach, dancing by herself long before that became popular, thin arms arched over her head, bare toes kicking up sand, face tilted to the moon, whatever guy she happened to be with that night shuffling along bewildered behind her. Once she did the Charleston on the roof of someone's car, there were tiny dents in the metal afterwards. Lord. People who didn't know her thought Becky's dancing had something to do with a wild nature but that wasn't it at all. She needed to throw herself into things utterly and completely, and dancing was a way for her to do that, to lose herself and forget what had happened to her. I envied her that wild abandon, and still do.

But then it was Becky's wild abandon that did her in.

She was crazy in the way of girls from rich families. The Lord has spared me from that particular pitfall. Yeah, right.

In her final year at Red Rock High Becky announced she was getting out of town as fast as her boots would carry her. She had travelled to Winnipeg and Toronto, the latter on a teen fashion jaunt arranged by Eaton's department store for young women who showed promise in the modelling line. All the girls at school were weak with envy before she went, and when she came back with stories about Yonge Street, and with grown-up women's perfume dabbed on her wrists, we all had to do the same, to the horror of our mothers. Already Becky had a reputation, easily acquired in those days. Her boyfriends were guys who weren't in school anymore, guys our mothers warned us about, including Tommy Piper. Becky rode around in their cars after classes, smoking cigarettes and playing the radio loud, drinking beer from bottles and swearing like a sailor. She wore skirts cut high above the knee. When I told her what people were saying about her, she laughed and was like, "Who gives a rat's ass about a bunch of old biddies!"

I laughed along with her but I was frightened. Scarlet lipstick was one thing and skinny dipping on Saturday night another, but there were lines a girl didn't cross, not a girl who was thinking of any kind of a future for herself. Ann-Marie and I were virgins and we meant to keep it that way. We knew what had happened to Sylvia Stark, and if we'd forgotten for as little as one minute our mothers would have reminded us, but Becky went her heedless and reckless way.

Mother was like, "That girl's headed for trouble." She punctuated such statements by looking over the frames of her glasses, daring you to disagree.

And I went, "She's my friend."

"Which is my point."

"And she's not as dumb as you think."

"Or as smart as you like to believe, young lady."

"I know what I'm doing."

"Oh, that is rich."

I wasn't as sure of myself as I made out, but it was an unstated principle that you could not agree with your mother about anything, so you had to huff out of the room and leave her fuming until the next time she got a crack at you.

Mothers and daughters, you know how it is.

We lived on Spruce Road, we Cirinis, in a three-bedroom bungalow, while the Johnsons lived on Birch Crescent in a three-storey brick house, the most imposing in Red Rock, along with the other mine big-wigs, the Johnsons, the McCarthys, the Hancocks, the Beamans. These were people who came to Red Rock from big cities in the east, a lot of them Americans from the States. The Beamans came from Georgia and spoke in wonderful drawls, don't you know, honey. What a riot! Like the Johnsons and Hancocks they attended the Anglican church every Sunday.

Spruce Road was at the bottom of the hill, and between Birch Crescent, at the top, and those of us at the bottom was Maple Avenue, where the more prosperous businessmen and their families lived: Mel Noden and Arnold Piper, the United Church crowd. *Flash,* Mother called them. They drove new cars and took their families on motoring vacations to the States every summer and came back with exotic liquor, Jim Beam, and endless stories about the Grand Canyon and the Rockies, don't you know, sickening is what they were. We went to French Lake – and for a real treat, Port Arthur for a weekend. Most of us miners' kids were dragged off to Mass twice a week by our devout Catholic mothers, but there were lots on Spruce Road who didn't go to any church at all, even at Christmas and Easter. *The Godless,* Mother called them.

Hank Peterson was one of those. He was only in a church once, to my knowledge, the day of his wedding, and not even to have Scott christened or baptized when he came along. My Lord. But like the rest of us in our modest bungalows, he looked up the hill to Birch Crescent at the brick houses where Becky and her lot lived like kings and queens in our town. I don't suppose that he ever really thought one of the princesses would come down to him.

None of us did, actually.

And it would have better if she had not, that's a fact, but it seemed a wonderful romance at the time. Before it all went sour and turned the town in on itself. Because in one way what happened to Becky and Tommy and Hank marked the beginning of the end for Red Rock. Sure there were the strikes, the fights over the conveyor belts, the lay-offs, the vandalism, but mining towns recover from that stuff, it's their bread and butter. What happened with Hank and Becky was different. He was a poor boy who married a rich girl and then found it all snatched away from him, so he lashed back the only way he knew how, and the powers that be do not like that, they exact their revenge on little guys, they squash them like roaches.

I mean there was talk in the hotels before the trial that Hank would be run out of town by Sam Johnson and his lot just because he was a poor boy who had dared to touch the shining princess. That kind of talk got the miners' blood up. To them it was just another instance of the working guy getting stiffed by the bosses, it tore the town in half, in the end it took the heart out of our town.

But I get ahead of myself.

Now, when we were working night shift together at the hospital and hit the quiet slope just after midnight, we'd steal a smoke in the washroom. Becky liked to talk about our days in high school. She was like, "We had a riot, eh, babes?" She was only twenty-three but already living in the past, what with having the baby and all.

She forgot sometimes that everyone hadn't enjoyed high school the way she had. It wasn't just the boys and the popularity thing. I was not much of a student but my mother was absolutely sold on doing well at the books, forever pointing out that the only way to escape a town like Red Rock was to get a high school diploma. She believed that stuff about education being the key to success, bless her weary old heart. Up until my final year she hovered over my homework, making sure my math was done and the essays typed out. I understand her point now, but then we fought every night, mostly about Becky Johnson, who would be on the phone before we had finished supper, coaxing at me like a Jehovah's Witness to make up a foursome with her and some guy in a shiny car. Then followed a shouting match between me and Mother. "If Becky Johnson jumped off a bridge, would you have to jump too?" Mother would scream at me, I think because we both knew the answer was *yes*. Thank God she never asked me, Becky, that is, because I would have waded through a river of blood for that girl, sure enough.

By Grade Ten it was obvious she was going to be the star of our grade. She was on the dance committee and the cheerleaders. While the rest of us were hoping to be invited to the bush parties out at King's Throne, Becky had boyfriends in Grade Twelve who whisked her off the school grounds in their cars when classes were done and sat with her over Cokes at the Steep Rock Café until supper time, smoking and even necking sometimes, she showed me the hickeys. Lord. Her parents objected, but Becky just laughed in their faces. She wore tight skirts and red nail polish on her fingers and toes. After a party at the Standishes she'd gone upstairs with Arnie and hadn't got home until two. Her father had struck her with a belt, she told me, showing me a welt on her thigh. *The Old Bastard,* she called him. She bought "Great Balls of Fire" and played it on the phonograph in her bedroom at top volume until her mother shouted from the bottom of the stairs that she'd be grounded for a week if she didn't turn it down. It took my breath away when she went out to the top of the stairway and yelled down, "You just try, you old bag!" That was near the end of Grade Eleven when Billy Alexa was showing scratch marks on his back to the guys on the hockey team and claiming Becky made them with her nails in the throes of passion. Ann-Marie and I overheard that at a party and the way we looked at each other we could tell we believed it ourselves.

I'm just saying what I remember, and the memory can play tricks, right?

That summer Becky went to Toronto and when she returned in the fall she was changed, she smoked more and drank lemon gin mixed with ginger ale, *panty remover,* she called it. She called girls who didn't drink *pills.* She talked about condoms and pieces of tail. It made my blood run cold to hear it, such slutty talk. Then she took up with Johnny Armstead, and I drew the line myself at dating Indians, so we drifted apart. I was working hard to keep up my grades, staying after classes some nights for special tutoring. Mother's plan was for me to go to Port Arthur and train as a dental hygienist, but then she discovered she had cancer and all that changed.

For sure the transformation in Mother was remarkable. In a few short weeks she went from being a vigorous housekeeper and pesky parent to an invalid. She caved in, is what happened. The cancer was in her breast and she showed the lump to me one night after the doctors had told her about it. "I'm dying," she sobbed, tearfully, "I'm dying, Madgie."

After she told me and after we were done weeping I had to vomit. In the bathroom I sat with my knees on the floor and spewed my guts into the toilet, it felt like my womb was going to come out, too. The linoleum was cold. The porcelain toilet seat was cold, too, when I lay my forehead on it and wondered what would happen to us.

What happened was I ended up taking care of her. After I'd vomited some more I washed my face off and went back into her bedroom. I sat down beside her and stroked her arm. "Mother," I went, "it's going to be okay. I'm going to take care of you." She opened her eyes. She smiled weakly and squeezed my hand. She closed her eyes and sighed deeply. That's all she needed, the comfort of those words. "That's good," she whispered. And then she dropped into a deep sleep.

Taking care of Mother turned into a full-time job. What with going to classes and doing homework and shopping for groceries and so on, I hardly had time to talk on the phone to Ann-Marie or Becky, much less go to the parties and dances. Father was always like, "Get out with your friends, girl, and let your hair down a little," and I did manage it once or twice. But looking after Mother that year and in the years that followed I lost track of all the girls, Becky especially, and we weren't the friends we had been before. She slipped away from me somehow while I was taking care of Mother and then getting certified as a practical nurse, making a career out of what had started as a duty. And even after Becky married Hank and had little Scott and came to work at the hospital as a practical, too, we never really re-established our friendship.

So I missed my chance to save Becky Peterson. She slipped away from me: I knew what she needed but I could not give it to her because I was too busy with my own life, and I will never get over the guilt of that, and guilt, as they say, is what makes the girl go around.

There is one night, though, that I want to tell about.

Towards the end of our Grade Twelve year there were a number of graduation get-togethers, beach parties, school functions, and house parties among them. We were not just graduating; a number among us were heading off to college, leaving Red Rock for good. It was a busy time of speeches and corsages; of dancing, drinking, and tearful farewells. Boys who had never touched a drop got vomit drunk; girls who had kept their virginity all through high school found themselves suddenly ready to take the plunge, and some were none too picky about who with, truth be told. Still. The boys washed their fathers' cars and their girlfriends helped them decorate them with crêpe paper and bows. Becky had smashed up her father's Edsel a month earlier but we found ourselves in a gravel pit one night after a party, and we stumbled out of the car for fresh air when the guys who were our dates lit up cigars to go with their beers, a filthy habit, in my opinion, don't tell me about not inhaling, they all end up doing it, and the lungs get just as coated whether its stogies or cigs, only cigars being ten times as big there's that much more carcinogens built up in there. Awful.

But where was I, now?

It was a warm but dark night and when our eyes adjusted to the light all we could see was the car and the outline of the rock face looming some fifty feet above us. It was the floor of a gravel pit, wasn't it? We were looking up from the bottom of a hole. Becky was like, "Piss on this." We'd had a few drinks ourselves. She pointed towards the rim of the pit, indicating we could sit there and finish the lemon gin and ginger ale mixed in the soft drink bottle she was holding. We felt daring. We scrambled up the steep slope in the moonlight, scuffing our shoes and tearing our dresses and swearing, having a grand old time of it, though.

From the rim of the gravel pit we could see the highway leading out of Red Rock and the orange glow from the mines in the distance. We tucked our dresses up under us and sat in the rough grasses, dangling our feet over the edge and kicking gravel loose with the heels of our shoes. A couple of brats. Out on the slut. The stones rolled down the slope and a few tinked against the car. The guys had the radio on loud. Overhead the moon was a bright disk.

Becky drank some gin and passed the bottle to me. I drank a little and when I made to pass it back she shook her head, so I cradled the bottle in my lap. We sat in silence for a long time and then Becky sighed loudly.

I was thinking about my own future, how my ambitions were on hold, but I went, "You don't want to leave school, do you?"

It was the first time we'd talked in months and she kicked at the gravel for a while before answering. "Part of me does, part of me doesn't."

"I know, change."

"Christ, that's what I want. The bigger the better."

"I thought you were leaving."

"So did I."

"You for sure. We all thought Becky for sure is getting out. The Bombshell, all that."

"You don't know my father."

"He doesn't want you to?"

"Won't let me."

"But the Eaton's thing, the modelling –"

"He won't let me have the money, the cheap bastard."

We studied the mine road. Every now and then a car went past, but it was late, between two and four in the morning. My parents were letting me stay out the whole night, the first time ever.

"Fuck him." Becky reached over and took the bottle from between my legs, holding it up in the moonlight to see how much was left. When she'd taken a drink she went, "I'm pissed. I'm damn well pissed here."

"Me too."

"No, it's not the money." Becky snorted. "My father," she went on, "says I stay in Red Rock until I'm a grown woman, a lady. That's a laugh."

That wasn't such a bad idea, now. Becky had some growing up to do, in my opinion. "One year," I offered, "what's that?"

"The old bastard won't let go."

"My mother says –"

"Won't let go of me." She swallowed more gin. "Shit," she went, "who do you think you're fooling, girl?" Her head sagged down to her chest for a moment, like a drunk's, but suddenly she reared back and raised the bottle in the air and then smashed it on the stones, showering us with droplets of gin and sending shards of glass shooting past our faces.

My hands flew up in reflex. "Becky!" I yelped "Jesus!"

She glared at me.

Neither of us said anything for a few minutes. Finally I went, "What the hell's got into you, girl?"

She was like, "Fuck off."

I swallowed hard.

"Just fuck off, Madge."

I was like, "I'm your friend."

"Hoh, well, friend, I've got something to show you." She jabbed the broken neck of the bottle in my face, the edges of glass not an inch from my eyes, and when I gasped, she jerked the bottle away and stabbed the jagged points of glass into the wrist of her other arm.

I could see the glass puncturing her white skin.

She laughed. For sure Becky Johnson was crazy at that moment. She positioned the jagged glass in the middle of her tiny wrist and pushed down hard. Blood spurted from the veins, a tiny little arc that shot up about two inches before looping back onto her skin, like water in a tiny fountain. She looked at it and then into my face.

I was like, "Blessed Mother Mary...."

"Stop that," Becky snapped. "Stop that!"

Now, we were sitting close enough that she could reach me and she back-handed me in the face, which made me start crying and blubbering. We sat in silence for a while. Finally I went, "You'll hurt yourself, Becky. You'll kill yourself."

She laughed. "That's the idea."

I was like, "You need to go to the hospital." I started to rise.

She grabbed my skirt in her fist and jerked me

down, screaming, "Don't move, you little bitch, and don't call out or anything." She waved the jagged bottle at me. "Or I'll do the other."

I had sat down hard. "If we get you to the hospital…."

"I'm not going back there. Ever again."

"You'll bleed to death."

She held the bottle neck up to the moon and then she looked at her wrist, still trickling blood. "I deserve to die."

"You're crazy. Drunk and crazy."

"Don't be ridiculous." She stuck her chin out and inhaled deeply.

"At least let me staunch it." I was bunching some of my dress in my fist. She did not protest, and I held the wad of material over the wound, pressing down to stop the flow of blood, the way I'd seen in posters on hospital walls.

After a while she went, "I hate him, hate him."

"I know."

"No, you don't. That's what I'm trying to get through your thick head. You don't know a damn thing." She paused. "It has nothing to do with the money."

"I know."

"You don't know shit all! Listen for once, you stupid pill!"

"Look, Becky, there's been rumours since your mother took you away that time back in grade school. Everyone knows he – he hits you. Used to."

"I'm a laughing stock, you mean."

"Everyone feels sorry for you."

"Oh, yeah, like my own mom, the sorry bitch."

"If she can't do anything about it, how do you expect us to? Shit."

Becky spat over the lip of the gravel pit and we watched the comet of saliva drop into darkness. "What you don't know," Becky went, "is why he does it."

I waited for a moment for her to tell me and then ventured, "Boys?" I was still holding my dress tight against her wrist. The flow of blood had slowed to an ooze, but she had lost a lot of blood. That alone would have made her light-headed, much less the gin she'd consumed.

"That's a laugh." Becky was still holding the bottle neck in one hand and she flung it suddenly into the air. It arched in the moonlight for a second and then dropped to the floor of the gravel pit, smashing in the stones. "That's a total riot. Boys."

Below us the car headlights went on. One of the guys yelled, "Hey, you two still holding hands up there in the dark?" Both of them laughed but they did not get out of the car.

Becky pulled her injured arm away from my hand and held it up to the moonlight. The blood had started to flow again, but when she pressed her thumb over the wound, it stopped. "I meant what I said," she whispered, "about deserving to die."

"You're confusing me."

"I know, sorry." She sighed and kicked at the gravel for a minute or so and then went, "What I'm telling you, you have to promise never to repeat."

"Okay."

"Promise." She studied me. In the shadowy light

her eyes looked as if they'd disappeared into her skull, but two pinpoints of intensity glimmered through. "Say after me...."

"I promise never to repeat it."

"Good, that's right." We sat in silence for a while. It was a warm spring night and a light breeze was soughing through the trees. Becky cleared her throat. "It's because," she went, "he's done it to me." She let that sink in. "Yes, when I was a girl, lots of times, right in my little bed, ugh it was awful." She hung her head. "Christ, I'm ashamed to admit it." When I reached out my hand to her, she pushed it away. She took a deep breath and spoke in a calm, clear voice. "But not for a long time now. Thank God, not for a long time. But that doesn't matter to him, which is the point I'm trying to make to you. He's afraid, see, that's why he beats me. When I was young he was afraid I would tell someone so he hit me to shut me up, and now he's afraid I'll go away and, and I don't know what, get the cops on him, or a lawyer, or something." She sighed. "I don't understand how his sick fucking mind works, that's the problem. I don't know what he's thinking."

I was twiddling my thumbs in my lap and was like, "I'm sorry."

"It's okay, it stopped years ago. It's just –"

"You have to get out of there."

"It just frustrates me now. When I thought I'd get out. Was out."

"I know."

We sat in silence and then she whispered, "Listen, that's not all." She inhaled deeply, exaggerating her anguish. "One afternoon a month or so ago I tried to kill myself." She paused and we listened to the wind in the pines. "That's right, I'd be dead now if it hadn't been for plain bad luck." She inhaled and plunged on. "I got his shotgun out of the basement and went up to my bedroom and put the barrel into my mouth. I'd written the note already. I was in a desperate mood. Awful really. I sat on the edge of my bed and pulled the trigger. You may find this funny. I do now. Nothing happened. The gun had not been loaded. I sat there for a while, resting the shotgun across my knees and then scurried back downstairs, but by the time I found the shells and got upstairs, mom came in from shopping and I just couldn't do it with her in the house."

I didn't know how much of her story to believe but I was like, "Oh Becky, how sad, how awful."

"I'm okay now. The black mood lifted a few days later and I haven't felt that way again. Somehow, after I heard that trigger click... I don't know how to put it exactly." She laughed. "I'm back to being happy old me."

I let some time pass and then asked, "How could you do it? I mean hold the gun in your hands that way, actually do that?"

"Once the mood was on me it seemed easy. Doing it is just a matter of steps. You position the gun on the floor, you stick the barrel in your mouth, you reach down and pull the trigger. It took only seconds."

"That's not what I meant."

"No, you're wrong. It is what you mean but you don't get it because you've never been there. You imagine there's some great crisis of conscience to get over, like Hamlet, sweating and fretting it out in your mind, something like that. But once you are in that black pool you just do whatever comes to hand."

"Like stab yourself with a broken bottle."

Becky laughed. "It's not the same thing. Not at all."

I kicked at the gravel. "You're not okay, Becky. Not really."

"I am." She looked out at the road and took several deep breaths.

I studied my hands again. They were stained with dried blood, the way the hands of the miners were when they came into the hospital direct from the pits. My dress was ruined, too. I wanted to tell Becky a lot of things: that I was sorry for her, that I would stand by her, that she should see a psychiatrist, that she had to get out of his house and out of Red Rock whatever the cost, but I could not say any of those things. I was afraid she'd swear at me again. Girls are so easily hurt. I thought she would laugh at me, so I kept my trap shut, but I swore a silent oath to myself that Becky Johnson would not stand alone from that day forward. I would take her to the hospital and get her wrist fixed. I would work on her about seeing a psychiatrist. Starting the next day I would talk to her every day and help her escape from Red Rock. I was filled with fine ideas.

But I was saying about Tommy.

He was hardly breathing when we hooked him up to the oxygen, and he was covered in blood from neck to feet. We removed his shorts from his body and wiped the worst of the blood off right away and applied compresses to his wounds. He was unconscious but moaning, wasn't he? We took his blood pressure and pulse. Doctor McCabe shook his head when we told him what Tommy's diastolic was. He muttered something in Latin I didn't quite get and we prepared the injections and intravenous.

It was maybe eight o'clock by then, what should have been the end of my shift. There had been a half hour gap between the ambulance going out and its return, and during that time the corridors of the hospital had surged with rumour and speculation. Rhonda Beaulieu, who took the call from the Petersons', thought all three of them had been shot dead. Somebody got the idea Scottie had been shot too. Someone else said Tommy and Becky were dead and Hank had fled town in his car, the cops behind him in a high speed chase. I thought it unlikely that Hank would have fled the scene, given his character, but given his character I would not have believed him capable of shooting anyone either. Alice Dawe, Dixon's girl friend, who later became his wife, and who was our supervisor on the graveyard shift, was called to the phone and spoke to him, and we all expected her to be able to throw light on things, but when she returned to our working station and we gathered around, she had no information to offer, either.

I thought of how in the years that had passed since our graduation I had talked to Becky only a half-dozen times and then in the way of light-hearted work place banter, never anything serious. She steered conversations clear of her family. She had never mentioned that night at the gravel pit again. She wanted not to remember it, and I was afraid to bring it up. I was also very busy with Mother. Father had bought a colour TV, and the dancing pictures of Lucy and Desi occupied her for several hours a day, but what she needed most was personal attention: endless games of Crazy Eights and Canasta; walks down to the river; chit-chat over cups of coffee. Her colour had come back but she was weak. While she was taking the treatments I sat in the waiting room for hours. Ah well. The Lord blesses those who only stand and wait.

So Becky and I drifted apart and I never did live up to my vow to look after her.

Now, she was on my mind a lot. When she didn't leave Red Rock the fall following graduation, she started coming into the hospital as a volunteer. I'd see her making beds in one of the wards or cleaning up in the reception area. It seemed exactly the kind of work Becky Johnson should not be doing, the princess from Birch Crescent, getting her hands soiled with other people's body fluids, breaking nails on bed pans. I had expected to find her behind the cosmetics counter at Eaton's and was surprised, shocked, that I hadn't, but now it makes perfect sense that she wouldn't want to be reminded every day of how she'd fallen short in the career she aspired to. Or maybe she needed to be cleaning things, a kind of penance. Who knows? She was fidgety, though, and smoked with a vengeance. It was clear that she was looking for something and likely it was spelled trouble. When I saw her around town it was always with some guy and usually a different one each time. She wore lots of eye makeup and scarlet lipstick. She laughed at the end of every sentence she uttered, a high nervous little tinkle that was supposed to indicate how carefree and happy she was, but actually revealed fear and insecurity. Her hands and feet never stopped moving.

Now, that was just about the time Hank Peterson arrived in town. He was a bit of a bantam rooster, puffing up his chest and looking about to see who was taking notice, but that was a little affectation, and no more. At heart he was just a nice guy. I liked him from the moment we met, at a dance at the Union Hall, and I imagined for a short period he had taken a fancy to me, too. After the eager boys of high school with their restless hands, Hank seemed gentle and kind. He danced in a clumsy, off balance way that made him more endearing than the smooth dancers with their shiny shoes and slick hearts. He was good-looking besides being a nice guy, and women liked him.

He was the opposite of Becky in the sense that he seemed content with who he was. After her dizzy ride through high school, after her hopes about escaping Red Rock had been dashed, she was looking for a place to rest, a shoulder to lean into, a man to love her in a quiet, unassuming way.

What I'm saying is Hank was good for Becky, but she should not have married him.

What Becky Johnson should have done was shelter in Hank's embrace for a month or two, and then gone on to burn off whatever demon was eating her up inside before getting married. That's what her restless soul needed. Not marriage. She needed at least ten years of craziness before settling down with a man like Hank. During that ten years she should have hooked up with the kind of man she found in Tommy Piper, someone impulsive and careless and filled with boundless sexual energy, untrammelled by scruples and guilt, but a whole lot of fun, bless his foolish young soul.

Oh, the night of the hospital Christmas party, let me just tell about that.

It was one of those blow-out things, end of the year wing-ding, too much drinking, let your hair down, lampshade on the head after months of tension and stress affairs.

Anyways, Becky. She wore one of those skimpy little shifts she liked so much, hemmed six inches above the knee, strapless, cleavage. The men talked about her breasts, but I always thought her legs were her best feature, went all the way up to her ass, as someone said. Lord. Of course Becky couldn't help flirting. Then sometime around midnight she asks me to stand guard outside the coatroom, she's going in there and not to powder her nose, wink-wink.

I haven't the foggiest who it was.

But after a while it was like hiccoughing in there, loud, not gasps so much as a kind of choking. She was always dramatic, Becky. Then one sharp cry, like the cats make in summer under the hedges. When Becky came out a few minutes later she took me by one elbow and steered me to the bar, in the reception area. Rum and Coke was thick on her breath. Her hair, though, was just the same as when she went into the coatroom, her scarlet lipstick perfect. She squeezed my elbow. "Happy New Year," she whispered, and laughed.

It was shortly after that that she said to me, "You don't really like me, do you? You think I'm a tramp." Strong words, even for Becky.

"It's not that," I said, "but I would never do what you've done, being married and all, going with other men."

"That's just the point," she snapped, "you're not hitched. You don't know what you're talking about. If you were in my shoes, you'd probably be on your back with a different guy every night."

"No," I said, "I wouldn't sleep with another man, if I had made vows to someone I called *husband*. Not for all the world."

"Ho," Becky said, "ho ho." She gave me one of her long looks. "That is where you're dead wrong, kiddo. Because for the whole world it would be worth it."

"No," I protested. "Not to me."

"Because then the whole world would be at your feet, right? You'd be the Queen or something and could have people's heads chopped off if they said a bad word about you. And who would dare say you'd done something wrong then? No, sister, for the whole world it would be entirely worth it."

You couldn't argue with that kind of twisted logic, but you could say she had it coming. "Happy New Year!" indeed.

So. I felt sorry for Tommy as we set to work on him. He was a good-looking guy, if a little wild, and I felt he'd had a raw deal from life. You're not supposed to do that, have feelings, they get in the way of judgment, you're told during training. I don't believe that, as I've never swallowed holus-bolus ninety per cent of the advice doctors dispense along with the prescriptions they write. Healing the human body is a complicated business, and the more that goes into it, the sympathetic reactions of doctors and nurses included, the better, in my opinion.

After administering pain killers and hooking Tommy up to the drip, we started in on blood transfusions. His blood pressure was dangerously low. Stabilization is what you're after when somebody is as messed up as he was. We could tell Tommy was on the edge, and there's a nervous tension to every move you make in those conditions. Doctor McCabe closed up the two or three big wounds immediately, stitching rapidly to stem the blood flow. He had been a surgeon in the war and knew how to triage and buy time. Then he attended to as many of the superficial wounds as possible, plucking pellets from the areas of the back where the shotgun blast had struck. He sutured quickly. We kept an eye on Tommy's vital signs and cleaned and washed the areas Dr. McCabe had worked on. It looked like he might pull through, though it was also clear he was unconscious and might remain so for a long time.

His entire being, as they say, was in deep trauma.

Dr. McCabe seemed more hopeful as time went by, glancing at the clock on the wall from minute to minute. He would have to decide whether to perform the surgery on Tommy's major wounds or move him to a larger hospital.

I was wondering when we'd see Becky wheeled in. There had been a hushed conversation between the ambulance guys and Doctor McCabe after they'd moved Tommy to a hospital gurney, and I suspected she was already past help, but I prayed it was not so. This was my chance, I thought, finally, my chance to demonstrate I'd meant that vow at the gravel pit.

She had died, we heard later, almost immediately. The Lord is merciful.

At the trial, now, I sat in the back row, sometimes among the reporters who flocked to town to cover the big scandal. They got it all wrong: Becky, Hank, Tommy, the people of Red Rock. Mother read every item she could get her hands on, and then insisted on reading the juicier bits aloud to me. She couldn't muster the strength to sit in court, but she had the radio and TV, too.

Hank was calm. He wore a white shirt with a tie

and jacket every day, and he seemed uncomfortable in those clothes, as if his neck and shoulders were pinched in and bunched up and he was all constricted inside. He listened impassively when the lawyers made statements to the jury and when various people gave their testimony, most nervous and sweating under the eyes of the judge flown in from Toronto to hear the case. Sometimes when someone was testifying, Hank's lawyer leaned toward him and whispered a question and then they nodded and conferred in whispers, Hank tight-lipped, his lawyer running his tongue round his lips as he took in Hank's words. From time to time Hank sighed aloud and you had to wonder what was going through his mind.

Maybe he was thinking of what he'd done and regretting it. Maybe he was sorry and needed a priest. Maybe he was thinking of Scott and if they would be able to pick up the pieces of their lives when the trial was over. Maybe he was just bored. I know I was some of the time. I thought then of what had got them into this mess in the first place: of how quickly Becky had married Hank after they had started dating, and of how opposed to it her parents had been. That's why she did it, I see now. It served her purposes: she got out from under her father's hateful presence by doing exactly what he most feared, running off with another man, a miner at that.

The wedding was small and hurried. I remember Becky phoning to invite me, whispering in a low voice, conspiratorial, still a schoolgirl at heart. Her parents, she explained, thought Hank was too old: she was about to turn twenty and he was twenty-five. They didn't like the fact that he was just a miner, etcetera, etcetera. It pleased her no end that she was defying them. The way she talked, getting married to Hank was a game that let her get back at her parents for all the stuff they'd done to her. Some women are like that.

She wore a white dress with a shallow scooped neck and short full skirt, not the traditional wedding gown. The ceremony took place in the United Church. The vows were brief and the guest list briefer. I gathered from something Becky said that she would have preferred no one at all, including her parents. I felt sad, looking around the near empty church, but Becky was a picture of joy, beaming smiles, holding Hank's arm, dipping her nose into the bouquet she held in one hand. When they came out on the church step after signing the registry, Becky let out a loud whoop and tossed the bouquet into the air with a laugh. She was like, "*Misses* Peterson, it's crazy, kiddo." We threw confetti, we tied tin cans to the car with a piece of binder twine, and then they were off to a motel outside of Port Arthur.

The Johnsons had refused to put on the usual wedding party and dance. They stood silently in the background, thin smiles frozen on their faces.

Hank took everything in stride. He smiled, he posed for the cameras, he stood with a knot of the hockey guys on the curb and laughed at jokes before he and Becky climbed into the car and sped off. I wondered at the time if he knew what he was getting into. I thought he didn't, but now I'm not so sure. He had that passivity about him that can be mistaken for blindness until you realize one day it is just a quieter way of going about getting exactly what you want, dogged as a pregnant sow. Hank was not the fool some people thought. He knew what Becky was and what she had been. He liked her that way: it made her sexy, and there was a part of him that craved that.

But he drew the line at carrying on with other men. I don't blame him.

She was trying to provoke him, I see that now. It was the same as when she took up with all those different guys after high school – miners and Indians – and then married Hank at the drop of a hat because she knew it would drive Sam Johnson crazy. Becky hated herself. She was pretty and vivacious but when she looked in the mirror she saw trash, she saw a girl who let her father use her and was soiled and ugly and deserved to be punished for being the sewer hole she had become. In her own opinion she was a slut, a little whore, the worst imaginable thing for a girl to be.

Everything she thought was wrong. I knew it even then and I felt sorry for her being so down on herself, but I did not see the whole picture then. I did not understand that her carrying on was part of her sickness: that she needed a kind of apocalyptic cleansing, something that would wash the stains off her, the burden of guilt she carried around on her bird-like shoulders.

Ah well.

She had learned how to get that cleansing from her father easily enough. Over the years she had learned how to provoke him, and though those beatings must have torn her up inside, she kept provoking them in order to bring the whip down on herself, which made her feel clean in a weird way.

God, it's a messed-up world.

After she married Hank, Becky was okay for a while, but then the need to hurt herself, to be hurt, surfaced anew, so she flung herself at Tommy Piper, knowing Hank would find out, wanting him to, and yearning deep inside for the punishment. It was a cry for help, wasn't it? When Hank walked into the house that morning, part of Becky must have heaved a sigh of relief. The cleansing was at hand. I see it that way now. And this, too. After Hank had shot Tommy she screamed at him. She was not pleading for mercy, she was white-hot with anger, but not because Hank had discovered them – because he had shot the wrong person. *Kill me,* she must have screamed at him. *Me.* And when he looked at her, blank and uncomprehending, because he was expecting an apology, not anger, he was expecting her to prostrate herself before him, she screamed more hurtful words at him until she succeeded in provoking him: he was driven to distraction by her screams and by what he'd done to Tommy and did pull the trigger. Yes. For sure. But some minutes elapsed, seconds, I know it. I know Hank did not shoot right away and when he did he did not fully understand what he was doing. He had time between the two shots to figure it out, but he did not, the simple idiot. He did not see what Becky had done in screwing around with Tommy was a cry for help. He was not smart enough to get it.

It's only Hank I want to tell about now.

He did not say anything for the record throughout the trial. His lawyer sat beside him at a table during the proceedings. They conferred in whispers behind cupped hands, but when the time came, it was the lawyer who did the talking. Like most people, I thought the case would turn on one decisive piece of evidence that would demonstrate Hank's guilt or innocence once and for all. But I was wrong about that. Hank's fate, it turned out, hung on his lawyer's ability to undermine the testimony of the witnesses and confuse the evidence to the point where the jury was not certain what had occurred that morning, and so could not say *beyond a reasonable doubt* that Hank was guilty. It was a masterful strategy and worked to perfection. Sitting in the court room listening to Lyle Butler and Roy Buechler tell their stories and then become tangled up in uncertainty and perplexity under cross-examination from Hank's lawyer, I began to wonder if Hank really had gone into that bedroom that morning. So did the jury members by all accounts, and that's all Hank's lawyer needed to get him off. They called it temporary insanity.

I admired the man. He looked to be in his late forties. He wore dark blue suits and striped ties, yellow and green some days, blue and red on others, but the red was never more than a hint of colour. His dark hair was cut short and neatly combed. He spoke in a quiet voice, even when putting pointed questions to witnesses, and when he moved over to the jury box to direct his comments to the jury members, they leaned forward to catch his words. He held their attention by saying *consider this* and *do not forget that.* He hazarded little jokes sometimes, but not at the expense of witnesses, who he always addressed in the most respectful tones. He never once mentioned Hank's name, and there were whole days when you forgot the trial was about him, which was the point, I see now.

During one of the lunch recesses Hank stayed in his seat for a while, looking weary of the proceedings. It had been a long morning and I was a little spent myself. After a few minutes he glanced around and when he spotted me smiled. When I smiled back he lifted one hand from his lap and waved the tiniest wave imaginable. I rose and stood behind him, conscious of other eyes on my back.

"Madge," he went, "how like you." Up close I saw the dark pouches beneath his eyes and the creases at the corners of his mouth.

"It's been a long morning."

"How like you to come forward." His eyes looked up to mine. "It's been weeks since I've talked to any one except my lawyer."

"You've got a good one there."

"No one else has had the courage to just walk up and say hello." He smiled. "Imagine that, being afraid of me, being afraid to talk to me."

I was holding a hand bag over my stomach. I glanced down at my trembling hands and smiled. "Me too, I guess."

"It's the newspapers, they're making me out to be some sort of I don't know what, *monster,* I guess."

"No one pays any attention. People from around here know better."

"Do they?" It didn't sound as if he were that interested.

"They know you, Hank."

"The difference is, you came forward." He took a deep breath. "I want you to know, Madge, how much I appreciate that."

"It was nothing."

"Courage is everything. Without it, a person cannot go on."

"I guess." I thought for a moment about Mother and then for another about Tommy, who had lost his legs and the use of his voice and all memory of the recent past, according to the specialists in Winnipeg.

Hank went on, "I've had time to think and I know that."

I could tell by the way his eyes shone as he said it that it was true. We're in the habit of forgetting the simple virtues. I asked, "Have you heard anything about Scott? How he is?"

"They haven't let him come to see me. They haven't even sent word." Hank closed his eyes and took several deep breaths. "Like I'm contaminated or something. Crummy, isn't it?"

"It is. Just that. Crummy."

"Well, I miss the little guy."

"I know."

"He had just learnt to ride a tricycle."

I cleared my throat. "I'll try to find out and send you word. Okay?"

"He's a cute little fellow, isn't he?"

"I'll send word. I will."

"I would really appreciate that."

"All right, and you, you…."

"I'll be all right, I will." He held my eye for a second or two and then looked down, letting me escape without having to come up with an excuse.

So at home Mother was like, "That's a bad idea, writing to him."

"It's just a note. Telling him how Scott is. He misses his child."

We were sitting at the kitchen table, having a break from Crazy Eights. Mother was drinking coffee. She had been in good spirits for a couple of weeks even though she was losing weight again. Mother grunted. "I haven't seen Allan around lately."

I'd been dating several men off and on since high school, Allan Sutton among them, nice guys but somewhat dull, in my opinion. *Drips,* Becky called them. *I haven't had time Mother,* I wanted to bark back at her, *I'm chained here at home with you.* Instead I muttered something about Allan working a lot of extra time at the office.

Mother sipped at her coffee. "You'd think," she went after a moment, "you'd have stopped carrying the torch for him by this time. But I suppose this business just lights up new hope in you."

"What are you talking about, Mother?" I was sealing up the envelope with the note explaining that Scott was happy and feeling fine. I'd spoken with Kelly Spelchak, who was looking after him at the Johnsons' house.

"I am talking about you, about the fact my daughter has never quite given up on Hank Peterson."

"What? You're crazy."

"No," she went. "But either you are, or you're even

more blind to your feelings than I thought." She was tapping the pack of cards on the table top and revolving them in her fingers.

I was like, "Mother!"

She laughed, a gentle hollow sound. "Don't tell me," she went, "that you were not aware of it? How infatuated you've been?"

I could feel my face flushing. "Maybe at one time...."

"You're blushing," she went.

"Maybe when I was a girl."

"I haven't seen that in a long while, you blushing." She chuckled, then reached her hand across the table and covered mine. "It's okay," she went. "I promise not to tease you. I don't think Becky knew, either. Not really. And I won't tell your father. I just never realized."

"Go on, Mother."

We played another game of Crazy Eights and drank more coffee. All the while my mind was awhirl, going back over things that happened in high school, the times I'd been with Hank when he first came to Red Rock, the way I felt the day Becky and Hank got married, my weakness for little Scott, the lies I'd told myself about the guys I was dating, the way my heart flipped when I saw Hank on the street. What fools women can be. I played out the card games with Mother, but I was telling myself that it was time I grew up. Up to that moment it had been my opinion that Becky was the immature one, the one blind to what was really good for her, but

Mother had suddenly brought it home to me that I was the idiot for harbouring some school-girl fantasy about Hank sweeping me off into a romantic scene while a decent man like Allan Sutton waited patiently on the sidelines of the life I was screwing up. I was lucky Allan was still around, I told myself. Most women who were as silly as I had been spent a lifetime regretting it.

I remember looking up from my cards at Mother several times that evening and smiling at her. She was not the dummy I'd once thought, and I was glad I'd come to that realization before she died, so I could let her know in ways that she would understand. I resolved to do that.

I resolved, too, to bring Allan around to the subject of marriage again and to take him up on his hesitant proposal of a few months earlier. I wanted kids, I realized. It was time for putting certain things behind me. I'd learned a lot of things from what had happened to Becky and Hank and I realized the most important was that my life would be one of quiet, serene contentment. I was happy for that. At Port Arthur the previous summer I'd ridden on a roller coaster and I hadn't liked it one bit. I'd thrown up, truth be told. I understood then why. Roller coasters were for the Becky Johnsons of this world, not the Madge Cirinis. The Madge Cirinis wanted slow walks along the river and long, quiet evenings playing Canasta with cups of tea at our elbows. I saw my days rolling out in front of me like a straight, flat road: kids, a big old station wagon, mortgage, the golden wedding anniversary, bus tours of the Rockies, grey hair, grandkids. I would be the tortoise to Becky's hare. I couldn't wait to tell Ann-Marie, who was married to an accountant in Winnipeg and had sent me a postcard a month earlier, saying she was pregnant with her second.

Justifiable Homicide

Pete Dixon:

Listen, I know what this town thinks about me, says about me, and always has. *Jerk, creep*. I hear it muttered on the streets every day by folks shouldering past in too big a hurry to say hello, my neighbours, in theory. It was much worse decades ago when I first took this job. But still when I dare to venture into the Rockland for a glass of beer I hear the mutterings, just out of hearing but meant to be heard, if you catch my drift. *Prick, asshole.* You can't help but hear them, and, buster, I'll tell you one thing, it hurts to take that laying down. And another thing: the same ones got so much to say out the sides of their mouths in the Rockland are the first to come running when some blood gets spilled in their lives, they need a cop to mop it up. So what am I saying? I'm saying this is no easy job at the best of times.

Then some babe gets caught cheating on her old

man and all hell breaks loose.

I'm saying you try walking around in my boots for a week and then tell me how much fun it is being a town cop. Believe me, there ain't one in ten would do what I do at twice the pay. One in a thousand, more like.

I walk with a limp because of it.

My day starts at eight in the morning and ends at four in the afternoon, as often as I can arrange it now – or starts at four and ends at midnight, when I can't. Avoiding graveyard, you could say. I like those hours, but it's not the usual set-up for town cops, who normally work twelve-hour shifts with a day off every third rotation. Here's the thing: I've set it up so my time on duty matches exactly the miners' shifts. That way I'm getting up and going to sleep in the same rhythm they are, so I see the world the same way they do, have the same thoughts as them, and so on down the line. That's an advantage. It keeps me from making certain kinds of mistakes.

Mistakes are what this job is all about. Nobody realizes it but cops spend their lives picking up on other folks' screw-ups. Picking up on and picking up after. The guy who had this job before me said to me I don't know how many times, "Just keep your eye peeled for the unusual, Dixon, and you'll do all right." That's the long and short of it. Mistakes: in judgment, in calculation, and in timing. Everything I do involves someone else's goof-ups. Show me a good cop and I'll show you a man with a sharp eye for spotting mistakes.

Take robbery. You catch robbers, if you catch them

at all, because they screw up their timing. Somebody hears them breaking in, someone who should have been asleep or in another place, at least that's how the robbers figured it. That person calls the cops, then we bust our tails over there and Bob's your uncle we nab them. Not because we're clever like Sherlock Holmes and pick up on clues and track bad guys down by checking out fingerprints or tracing match book covers with addresses scribbled on. That stuff's for books. Who's got time for that? Maybe some Nancy boy in a starched shirt spends the rest of his life smoking a pipe and playing a violin. But not a real flesh-and-blood cop, one whose job is to cruise the streets nights, hustle drunks into the tank, fill in reports, keep track of time in and time out so the constables get paid, and all the rest of it, that's a cinch. Sometimes, yes, you stumble on a piece of dumb luck out in the cruiser car and you *spot* some poor slob breaking into a place and just nab him. That happens, I'll grant you. But mostly it's just picking up on mistakes.

Tommy Piper, now, there's a guy whose whole life up to the time he got shot was one big mistake, and though he's been hanging around now for thirty years and more, those mistakes have stayed with him – there's a lesson in that. I've known Tommy since he was a kid wearing a ball cap and spitting sunflower seeds, so I know what I'm talking about. Listen, that kid was bad news from the word go. In grade school he poured sugar into the gas tanks of three cars one Gate Night. That's what they call the night before

Halloween around Red Rock, a night when the same kids come knocking on your door for treats on Halloween reckon it's their right and privilege to play pranks on you, soap your windows, throw tomatoes against your house, and, in the case of Tommy Piper, screw up the fuel system of folks' cars so bad it costs them fifty bucks to get it fixed over at Noden's. Not my idea of a prank, buster. Don't get me wrong, I'm not against kids having harmless fun on a fall night, that's what Halloween's all about. But you ask me, it's two-faced for kids to destroy a man's property one night and then come round the next begging for candy. Be a man, I say. You want to destroy my property, go ahead give me your best shot and I'll be waiting for you in the shadows with my twelve gauge loaded with salt, let's see who comes out the better. But play fair. Don't come around the next day expecting us to be friends, two-faced, like.

That was Tommy to a T.

In school it was one jam after the other. Mostly to do with drinking, you get right down to it. Grade Ten, Grade Ten mind you, not even sixteen yet, not even legal for a driver's license, I find him in the high school parking lot one morning past 2:00 AM, lights on high beam and radio blaring. A neighbour heard the noise and then saw the lights, that's how the call came in. Like I say, mistakes. When I arrive on the scene, Tommy is weaving about the parking lot in bare feet, a half-empty mickey of rye in one hand, a book of poetry in the other. Poetry, Jesus. He had a white shirt on, did I say that – and a tie! "Get a load of this," he says to me and starts in reading, like I was a book nut or something. Not another soul around. I says to myself, I says, there's a girl in this, some little skirt Tommy was getting into, hiding in the bushes or behind the corner of the school, scared as a mouse wondering how she's going to get home, but when I looked, no one. First he reads to me, *at* me I should say, something about a horse in the woods in the middle of winter, while I'm trying to reason with him and get him into the squad car. Then he vomits. Not on me, thank Christ, but all over the side of the squad car, an unholy stink, let me tell you, the entire next week. You know how the stink of a skunk hangs around your car when you run one down on a country road? All the time he's reading this poetry at me. Even after he's vomited and is wiping the stuff off his mouth with the tail of his shirt. I mean, can you beat that?

The worst of it is I have to drive him home to his folks. At least that first time I did, what with him being the Mayor's kid and the Mayor being my boss. Before we got there I pulled onto the roadside and walked him around in the air a little, trying to sober him up. That wasn't much use, the amount he'd guzzled back. He vomited again, and told me what I swell guy I was. Spouted out another ear full of poems. Then we got in the squad car and headed for his folks' place. I don't recall what happened on the steps of the Pipers' that night. It's blended in with a lot of other nights, the same in every respect, except the poetry. You see what I mean about this job.

In the years following it was everything from

drunk and disorderly to statutory rape. One night I'd be hauling Tommy out of the Rockland where he'd picked a fight with an Indian and the next I'm in some gravel pit in the middle of nowhere with a wee bit of girl crying on a mother's shoulder and her father showing me the blood stains on her panties. It got to the point where I heard his name, my stomach tied into a knot. One night I finally decided enough's enough, we're in a parking lot on the edge of town where Tommy has crashed a Euclid he hijacked from the mine, God knows how he got hold of that, into two or three cars, and I lay a beating on him, just to teach him a lesson in civics, you could say, try to put it into his thick head he's got to respect law and order around here. "Okay, Tommy," I calls out to him as I cross the lot toward him, "enough's enough. Time to talk man to man." I left my belt and pistol in the gravel along with my cap. Well, beating's putting it a little strong. Slapped him around a bit, say. Nothing that did any permanent damage.

Didn't do any good either. Kept the lid on the pot, you might say, for a while. I'd see him driving around town in that red Chevy his old man had to go and buy him, coon tail flying from the radio antenna like an advertisement. Which I reckon it was. I'm talking several years after high school, now, a year or so before the Hank and Becky business. By then he'd moved on from high school girls to the wives of miners, the net effect of that being to drop the count of statutory rape in our fine town but not the level of violence. No, Becky Peterson was not the first. What

I'm saying is Tommy had a couple of those lickings in back the Rockland coming to him. He'd been tom-catting around for some time before Becky, and doing pretty well, too, truth be told. I don't know what it is about men like Tommy, the broads just flock to them like bees to honey. What I'm saying is, I'm surprised someone didn't catch up to him with a gun before Hank did.

The puzzling thing was we'd come across each other in town, Tommy and me, and he'd always give me the wave and a big grin. He was a friendly kid by disposition and I reckon what you are as a kid doesn't change much when you become an adult. Human nature. Back in those days Tommy was a joker, a kidder, one of the boys. Here's what I mean. One Monday I came across him when I stopped in at The Steep Rock Café for morning coffee. This would have been before he started fooling around with Becky but after our little chat in the parking lot. He was sitting alone at a booth and when I walked past he gave me the usual wave and grin. One eye was black, half closed, a shiner. I stopped in my tracks. I'd had a few of those myself and knew how they felt. Your whole face hurts, you can't swallow coffee without pain knifing through your eye. I asked, "What happened to you?" not expecting an answer, really, but more as a way of passing the time of day. It's part of the town cop's job, keeping up friendly relations with the citizens.

"Well, now," Tommy says, "let me put it to you this way: I was talking to a guy when I should have been listening to him."

He wasn't always that funny. That night out at Dead Man's Curve was no joke. Like I say, Tommy was into the drink, and because he'd dropped out of high school the other kids kind of looked up to him. They saw him as a rebel, ducktail haircut, white T-shirts, a snotty attitude. Never understood that myself, but then I only got to Grade Ten before Korea came along and I was out in the real world, so what would I know about it? Anyways, I'd heard he'd go joy riding in that Chevy, revving the engine, spinning out in gravel, the usual teenage stuff, but I'd never caught up to him. Part of me was glad. I'd had a bellyful of strained conversations with Arnold Piper on his front steps. Back then the Mayor and me had our differences about what cops should be paid and the hours they're expected to work, so I didn't need to cross swords with him over his rotten kid every couple of weeks. Also I was counting on Tommy not being so stupid as to drink and then go chasing down the highway. The kids usually confined their drag races and joy rides to the straight stretches on the mine roads. My mistake.

By the time I got there Charlie Telfner was already dead, neck snapped, Doc McCabe said, by the impact of the car hitting the granite rock face. He'd been sitting in the death seat beside Tommy. Not a mark on him but dead as a door post. Maureen Regan was dazed, both legs broken. Pretty girl, Maureen, daughter of Ben Regan runs the Husky station on the highway. She's married now with two kids and only a slight limp, but that night we dragged her from the back seat, the ambulance guys and me. "Don't tell my dad," she's weeping, "don't tell him, please," like that was the worst could happen to a pretty young girl, her father knowing she was joy-riding with Tommy Piper. Shock does that. Two other kids in the back seats had facial lacerations and assorted bumps and bruises. Tommy was unscathed. To look at the car you'd wonder how any of them got out of there alive. The front doors were staved in, windows smashed, the hood folded back like an accordion, blood everywhere, even a big pool in the trunk. I'll tell you this, although it's unprofessional of me as a cop to say anything, I wished it was Tommy and not young Telfner stretched out on the front seat that night, mouth open like he was catching flies. Wished it then and wish it now. Tommy had it coming. Some do, and there's no point pretending it's any other way. None of that other shit would have occurred if it had been him died that night and not young Charlie.

People are right, I'm a hard case, but I'll say this, I feel sorry for his folks, Arnold, who as Mayor hired me way back when, and Nellie, who never quite adjusted to the fact that her boy was a bad apple, plain and simple, and went to pieces in the years he sat stone silent in a wheelchair at the General growing grey-haired, a paralytic with no voice box. Like I say, I wish the drinking was the worst of it. That I could have lived with. No, Tommy had this streak in him, like he was out to rub it in everyone's face what a crummy deal life had cut him. 'Course it hadn't up to that point, but we're talking here about how he saw it, not the facts of the case. I don't know what the psychiatrists call it but I call it Cry-Baby-Itis. The only thing that kid ever saw was how bad things were for Tommy Piper. Boo hoo, is what I say. Half the kids in this town would give their eye teeth to have it so good. What I say is, give me the house on Birch Crescent, the shiny bicycles, the brand new red Chevies, the trips to Chicago to see the Blackhawks, etcetera, etcetera, buster, I'll swap places any time.

That's because where I come from no one had a pot to piss in or a window to throw it out of. You're talking to a guy had a paper route at five, gas jockey at Melly's Shell when he was ten, roughnecking in the oil fields at sixteen, and into the Army two years later. It seems I've done nothing in my life but work. My older sister, the one married to that no-good ranch hand in Medicine Hat reckons he's a bronc-busting star of the stampede or something, has a theory about this: "Dixon," she says, "you never gave yourself time to be a kid, went straight from burping to bourbon." She could be right. I've never ducked my responsibilities. I've always taken care of myself by myself and done a pretty good job of it too, even if I do say so.

In consequence I don't have much time for whiners and complainers. The Army was full of them, you can take that to the bank. Belly-achers, we called them. Civilian life's not much different, except for the uniforms. I'm no philosopher, Christ knows, but the way I see it, this world's divided up into two kinds of folks, men and boys. Men go out there day after day, shit or no, and give it their best. Life's no parade and they know it. They put in an honest day's work, they respect the man, they take their lumps, they listen first and talk later. When they got a beef, men settle it fair and square and let the best man prevail. That way you can look yourself in the mirror come morning and have nothing to be embarrassed about. Boys, now, they make me sick. They are always trying to talk their way out of work, or anything unpleasant, for that matter, you can spot them by the wheedling voice. They talk like they know it all, too, but talk is cheap. The average joe can come off pretty smart when talking is all that's involved, but put him in a back alley with some punk's got a knife, you see his real colour. What I'm saying is, yellow. I've seen the rougher side of life and know what I'm talking about.

What I'm saying is, the true test of a man is what he does when no one else is looking.

You take Hank Peterson, now. I liked the guy. He was a friend, the only friend I had in Red Rock, but Hank was no saint. We went on these hockey trips every year, the MineKings, and those trips were an eye-opener. That's where you saw guys' real characters, when you took them away from their wives and their families and their jobs and bosses and put them in a situation where there was nobody looking over their shoulder. Here's what I'm getting at. Shorty Weir had a glass of rye and Coke in his hand before the train pulled out of the Red Rock station and he kept it topped up the entire time we were gone. Two weeks. Sleeper, hotel room, bar, it didn't matter. The only concession he made was drinking beer in the change room, before, during, and after games. But that was mild. Pete Flynn, our goalie, got loaded in the hotel one night and went walking on the cement ledge out the window. We were three storeys up. He made it as far as the room Dan Korvitz and I were in, three down from where he'd started. "Look," he called out to us, "I'm Tarzan, I'm flying." After he climbed in our window he started throwing the furniture out. By the time we had his arms pinned, two lamps and a chair lay on the ground below, smashed to smithereens. Don't get me wrong, I take a few beers myself, a few too many back in those days, truth be known, and I enjoy letting my hair down every once in a while, but I draw the line at throwing lamps out of windows and exposing yourself publicly. That's what Ed Nichols did in a bar one night, pulled his pants down and there he is fondling his dick through the fly of his boxer shorts. Jesus.

Hank was another story. On the ice he was usually Mister Nice Guy, give a hit, take a hit sort of thing, no offense, but occasionally someone gave him the stick and then his eye balls start spinning in his head, the sign he was out of control. One game that happened and the next time Hank and this guy who gave him the stick go behind the net, the other guy ends up on the ice with his face bleeding. No one saw exactly what happened but the other guy's nose was busted, straight across the bridge, both eyes black as pucks by the time they got his skates off.

You call that a mean streak and Hank had one, at least on the ice.

The Pus Doctor, someone dubbed Hank on one of our road trips, and it stuck. Ordinarily he was a level guy, smiling gently at jokes, getting beers out of the cooler for the guys who were playing cards. Ordinarily. Get him away from Becky, give him a few beers and something snapped. He was a different person. It was women. Hank loved women the way he loved country music and that was a bad mix. When we were travelling he liked to find a country bar and go dancing to see what stray bit of skirt he could rustle up. I'll give him this: he did a mean two-step. The women loved it.

He had a habit of picking them up in bars, definitely not a good idea when you're travelling through a town as a hockey team. In Calgary one time he found this drunk gal on the dance floor and in no time flat was headed out the door with her. That was about midnight, not the first time Hank had just taken off, so no one thought much about it. We didn't see him again until nine the next morning, a game day, when he stumbles into the hotel lobby, the knees of his jeans torn out, boots covered in mud, and shirt soaked through. This is the story Hank told. That broad was drunker than she looked, really smashed, but she insisted on driving her car, and a couple miles down the road hit the ditch, and rolled the car. Neither of them was hurt, but they were in the middle of nowhere. They hitched a ride with a cowboy in a pickup, who drove them to a gas station.

Hank went in to call the cops about the car and when he came out, the broad was gone and so was the pick-up. He took off across country, putting as much distance between himself and the scene as possible. The thing was, he had no idea where he was, and there was no one around to give him directions. So Hank spent the night stumbling through farmers' fields and crossing ditches and trying to hitch a ride back to the hotel.

That's just one Pus Doctor story. I don't tell it to run down Hank's character. Listen, the guy was my friend, he even phoned me a couple times from Whitehorse after he'd settled in there with young Scott. I tell it to keep things in perspective. Like most, Hank could go off the rails, is what I'm saying. Becky played around behind his back, and with Tommy yet, so she was little more than a little minx, no doubt about it. But I saw Hank do things most folks in Red Rock wouldn't believe. What I'm saying is, when the call came in that morning I was not surprised.

It was just about 7:30 and my shift was ending. Max McNult, my new constable, had broken the big toe on one of his feet fixing his car so I was doing his midnight to 8:00 that week, the shift I avoid if I can help it, but Billy Jewett had it the week before and fair's fair. I'd been watching the clock, I grant you that, waiting to go home for a shower and a long snooze. In those days Alice left for the hospital at 7:30, so there was no chance me dropping by on the way home for a quickie, but when the phone rang I thought it might be her, calling just to see how things had gone before my day ended and hers started. She's thoughtful that way, Alice.

Lyle Butler was on the line. He spoke fast, breathless-like, and at first I didn't get what he was saying and imagined there had been a break-in at the drugstore. "Dixon," he repeated in that sing-song voice sent shivers down my spine, "Dixon, there's two people been shot at the Petersons' place. Hank's got a gun."

Another thing about being a cop. You can't get emotional the way other folks do, can't afford the mistakes emotions cause. You have to think straight all the time, and to do that you practise being deliberate in your thoughts and speech, to the point where it sounds like you're retarded or something. Lyle, now, he gave me that information in a jumbled way, confusing, so I said to him calm as possible, "Slow down a minute. Who's been shot?"

Something I've noticed about speaking slow like that: you do it, and the person you're talking with starts doing it, too. Like yawning. "Tommy," Lyle said. I heard him taking a deep breath down the line, a good sign. "Tommy Piper is lying on the floor in a pool of blood and Becky is on the bed. Roy supposes she's dead."

"Roy Buechler's there too?"

"We heard the shots and ran over. You better get here."

"Okay," I said. "I'm out the door." My mind was in two places at once right then, sifting through the scraps Lyle had given me and reckoning what was the best way to inform Billy Jewett where I was –

leave a note at the station for him to find when he came in, or telephone once I got to the Petersons' – and I was so busy mulling that over, I forgot to tell Lyle not to move the bodies or anything else at the scene. My mistake. As it was, I wrote a note for Billy, reckoning I might get so tangled up at the Petersons' I'd forget to call in. I was right. It was Satan's own shambles over there.

On the drive over I says to myself, you could see it coming, Dixon, couldn't you? In the past month I'd noticed Tommy buying lemon gin at the liquor store and spotted his red Chevy coming and going at odd hours, sure signs he was on the prowl with some broad. One day I saw Becky in the drug store with the baby. She'd got a different haircut, and when I stood back and watched her, she wetted the tips of her fingers and dabbed them at her temples in front of the mirror Lyle Butler kept near the back of the store. She wouldn't be taking the trouble for Hank, reckons I, so who then? It didn't take me long to put two and two together.

Later everyone in town said I just can't believe it about the Petersons, not Hank, not Becky, they were such a fine-looking couple, so happy together, holding hands at the movies last week, etcetera, etcetera. You know how folks yammer on. Buster, I was not one of them. I'd seen too much to put my faith in anyone, much less a frippety little piece like Becky Peterson.

I'd turned on the siren and the dome light and was doing sixty through town. I was considering, too, the things that had to be done at the scene, checking the bodies and performing first aid, stabilizing the room for evidence, getting the crowd under control, making notes. I went over this list in my head a few times, hoping I hadn't missed anything. There's more to being a cop than waving a gun in the air, and with the siren blaring it's hard to keep your thoughts straight. That's when I remembered I'd forgot to tell Lyle not to move things at the scene, and I pounded the steering wheel for being such an idiot.

It crossed my mind Hank might be wandering the streets of Red Rock with a gun. Lyle hadn't said anything about that one way or the other, where he'd gotten to, I mean, and you don't want to get caught flat-footed where firearms are concerned, so I patted my police issue revolver, just to be certain it was on my hip. Not a Walther HP, the pistol I learned to fire in Korea, but a good piece, reliable works, and accurate within thirty yards. I hadn't used it but once or twice and not in over a year, but I took it out for target practice every month or so. I didn't reckon I'd need it this time either. Hank was most likely puking out his guts somewhere, but you never know where guns are involved. One thing I learned in Korea: it's on the day you least expect to kill someone that you end up pulling the trigger.

It was nearly fully light by then. The crowd was gathering on the sidewalk out front of the Petersons'. I cut the siren when I pulled up, jammed on my hat, and jumped out of the car, slamming the door just so everyone knew their representative of law and order had arrived. "Okay," I barked out, "back off the grass." What I mean is, the time for standing around hands in pockets was over. Someone has to take charge, is what I'm getting at. To do that you have to do a little shouting and shoving. Make yourself disagreeable.

Hank was sitting on the front steps with the Buechler kid. The first thing I did was get him inside the house and the kid home, where a kid belongs. Luckily he knew where the gun was, so the possibility of more damage from that quarter was eliminated right away, though the kid nearly made a hash of things by putting his prints all over the stock, the same way his old man and light-footed Lyle screwed up the evidence inside by wiping up the blood. The ambulance guys came in with me and threw the blanket off the body. Once we were sure Becky was dead, I had them cover her with a sheet, as per regulations. Then they stopped the bleeding from Tommy's body and hoisted him on the stretcher. I checked on Hank. He was stunned but not dangerous. I wrapped his shotgun in a towel and locked it in the trunk of the squad car. Things were moving along quick and clean, just the way I like. Luckily Lyle and Roy were out of the house, but by that time the damage was already done. I made Hank sit on the living room couch while the ambulance guys loaded up Tommy. I pulled the curtains shut so the stragglers couldn't see into the house.

I'll tell you this, Hank was one sorry sight. His hair was rumpled up like he'd just got out of bed, and there was a streak of blood running down his jaw. His hands were still dirty from work, stained iron red. Somehow his shirt, a miner's khaki work shirt, soaked through with sweat, had been pulled askew, so it looked at first as if he'd done the buttons up wrong, but that was just because the material had bunched at one shoulder and twisted. He sat stock still on the couch but his eyes leapt from one place to another. It was creepy in that house with him, I felt antsy the whole time. He looked tightly wound up and ready to spring at any moment. I kept my eyes and ears open. I had no intention of being jumped suddenly. The really weird thing is he kept saying "I'm thirsty," and "It's not her," and other things I couldn't quite catch the drift of. At first I thought he'd finally wised up to Becky's cheating little heart, but that wasn't it at all. Then I thought he'd been drinking, and when I leaned in close for a sniff, there was a whiff of liquor on his breath, but just a whiff – he'd likely had one stiff one before going into the house, but you couldn't say he'd been drinking.

That's, anyway, what I said at the trial, and it seemed to go down okay, though I don't like the way it fitted Hank's lawyer's argument about insanity. That morning he was no more insane that I was. And getting off by dint of that, I've always thought, made him look weak. Hank was a man and he did what any red-blooded man would have done in his place. Sure, he was a little shook up after, but what the hell, who wouldn't have been?

What I mean is, he stood suddenly and walked across the room straight toward me. "I want to say something," he says, coming up so close I could smell the sweat on his body. I put one hand on the butt of my revolver.

He was right in front of me by then, and stared into my eyes. We were about the same size and the same build, on the ice folks always confused us. Up close like that I could hear his lungs breathing in and out. The muscles in my arms tensed. I don't reckon he had a hot clue where he was or what he was doing, but it was creepy all the same, standing there staring like that. In the glow from the overhead light his skin looked yellow. Then something weird occurred. I felt for a moment like we were twins separated at birth who'd somehow stumbled across each other and weren't sure what to do, but could sense the similarity between us, not just in physical appearance but other ways, too, ways having to do with who we were way down deep in our skin, and what we might become. It was scary. I half expected a voice to speak out of the sky of something weird like that. And then the sensation passed. I was the Chief of Police in my blue shirt with the official crest and he was a miner in a khaki shirt who'd come home and found his wife in bed with another man and blown them both away.

I wanted to ask him about that, man to man, but he got the jump on me. Without moving his lips, without speaking it seemed, he asked, "Can you get me some water, Dix?"

We were standing near the bathroom, so I was able to oblige without taking my eyes off him, backing up like a crab and fumbling for the taps with one hand. When I handed the tumbler of water to him he said, "Dixon." That's all. He tipped the glass slowly to his lips and drank in a way that made me wish I had a glass of that cold water, too. Like it was the last water on earth.

The phone was in the hallway there, on a thigh-high table, and above it a cork board with photographs tacked to it. After drinking, Hank stepped over that way. He ran his finger around the edge of a photo that showed Scott in a blue sleeper thing with little white rabbits on it. "She didn't want the baby," he said. His voice was dry and nearly inaudible. I had to step closer to hear him. "They're a lot of trouble, babies," he said, nodding. He drank again. "A lot of work. We knew that before we had him but knowing is not the same thing as living with it day in and day out. You're up nights for the bottles and diapers, two, three times a night. You've got one ear tuned in even when you're asleep, listening for their little whimpers. You're tired every morning, dog-tired when you wake up, and it wears you down after a while, you get these black rings under your eyes and your ears ring from not sleeping. It's like graveyard. Then you have to watch them every minute of the day or they fall down stairs or shove things in their mouth and choke themselves. They're just a whole lot more work than you expect. She wasn't ready for that. But she loved him. She was a good mother."

I was shifting from one foot to the other, the way I do when Alice starts in about some procedure they've been doing at the hospital. I'm impatient, is what it is. I can't stand it when folks go on the way Hank was, rambling, leaping from one thought to another. I said, "Hank, I have to arrest you."

He nodded. "Look at him," he said, pointing to the photograph. "That's the sad part. She wanted to go dancing and take trips. They've got this club in the Lakehead, Mario's, cocktails and dinner and stuff. She loves the cha cha. They tie you down, kids do. You've got to make this decision before you even have them that your life is over." He was picking at his eyelash and blinking. "I'd made that decision and I thought she had too. Assumed she had." He picked at his eyelash and blinked again. It was driving me crazy. "Your life as a free spirit, is what I'm getting at, hopping in the car after work and driving to the Lakehead to dance, going skinny-dipping at Crystal Lake past midnight. Skinny-dipping, remember when we all did that? You just have to give that up. It's not that your whole life is over – just *that* life is over, that carefree aspect. I forced it on her, a high school kid. It was stupid and I was stupid. She needed something else, something besides being tied down to my notion of what our life should be. Does any of this make sense, Dix?"

"I've got the cuffs here," I said, "and I'm going to put them on – just for show – so folks know you're being treated just like anyone else."

"She said to me once, *There has to be more than this to life.* Shouted it. We were arguing. We were always arguing about going out at night and how much time

I spent coaching baseball and stuff. Her lips went all quivery when she was excited, did you know that? That's why she smoked. Kept her from getting the shakes, she told me. *There has to be more than this.* I was too stupid to see what she was getting at. But she was right."

"I've got them here. The cuffs. When you're done, put the glass down and hold your hands straight out front. Like this."

"Her mother thought she spent too much time reading those magazines. Put notions in her head. Made her unhappy. That wasn't it at all. She was just a girl who jumped straight from the prom to pushing a kid around in a pram. There should have been more for her. She had promise. She was prom queen, did you know that? She went on a course to Toronto to learn about being a model. Who wouldn't have felt the way she did? Who wouldn't have looked for some little bit of excitement?"

"Just leave the glass there," I said. I took it from him and put it on the table. My neck was sweaty. I felt the tag of my blue shirt digging into my hot skin. I wanted to smash that tumbler to the floor, I wanted to kick a hole in the wall, or to scream bloody murder, anything, I was so agitated, so fed up with Hank's stupid rambling. I took several deep breaths. *He's your friend,* I repeated to myself, *your friend.* About the time I'd finally got him to relinquish the glass, he put his hand out like he was going to pick it up again. "Leave it *there,*" I said. He pulled his hand back like a kid who's been slapped.

He looked at me, eyes blank as stones. "It's all clear to me now, but now it's too late. I should have done something to make it easier for her. I had my hockey and coaching and what did she have? A job that took up half her time, a baby crying through the night, and a dumb-ass miner for a husband, a guy who couldn't see past his own concerns." He shook his head. "The way I treated her," he said. He dropped his head and looked at the floor. "I didn't yell at her or beat her or any of that. I don't mean that." He looked at me. "Maybe it would have been better if I had."

"Some broads," I said, "it's just what –"

"No," he said. He shook his head. "No, I wasn't cruel. It was just – I – I neglected her."

When the cuffs clicked shut I asked, "Who did you shoot first?"

"She was a good mother," he said. "Real good."

"Him or her?"

"You know," he said. He'd been studying the cuffs on his wrists but he looked up at me then. "You know," he repeated, "I liked Tommy."

"Not me," I said. "He was a punk plain and simple."

"He was always laughing."

"He was out for himself alone. Look what his parents put up with."

"He was a happy guy. Happy."

"He made my life hell. And not just mine."

"Maybe that's why," he said, "when I pulled the trigger I suddenly lost interest in... " He was drifting off again, getting that look in his eye.

"Tommy Piper was a taker, is what I'm saying. If it had been me...."

"Dix," he said. "Is there more water?"

With the cuffs on it was a trick for him to grip the tumbler in both hands and tip it up to drink. He closed his eyes while swallowing, reminding me of Alice at communion. I was raised a Lutheran, gave it up when I left home, but Alice is a Catholic who won't miss the Mass. At first I hated it, the priests swaggering around in robes and mumbling Latin, the candles, the incense, all that. Then it grew on me. I began to see the point of the ritual, the point of doing the same things over week after week, year after year, century after century. It gave your life order, a sense of purpose beyond your petty concerns and problems. I liked the fact I couldn't understand the priest, I didn't want to, I had never liked being preached at by some well-meaning cretin wearing a white collar. Mostly I like confession.

My job is dealing with sin. We call it crime, but it's sin. One of the difficult things about being a cop is realizing you're never going to stop folks from being sinners. It's a hard lesson for a person raised a Protestant to learn. At first that's what you reckon you've been hired to do, so you run around trying to stamp sin out and feeling you've failed when you don't. After a few years it comes to you that it can't be done – folks are basically rotten, so they are going to murder and rape and rob and all those other things and you are helpless to stop it. You begin to feel like that kid with his finger in the dike. You drive yourself crazy trying to stop crime. What I mean is, setting it as your life goal to clean up sin and sinning. So what's the answer? The answer lies in having the right attitude toward sin, and that's where confession comes in. What I mean is recognizing that sin is with us and accepting it as a fact of life. Forgiving it.

Non-Catholics reckon that means saying it's okay to sin. But forgiving sin is not condoning it. That's what's so great about confession. It accepts sin and forgives it – providing you enter into confession in the right state of mind. For a cop confession is the great relief and the great release. Once he sees what it's all about, he can stop thinking he's responsible for sin and crime and purging the world of sinners. Like I say, that would drive you nuts. Chew on this for a moment: there's a reason so many cops are Irish Catholics.

What I'm saying is, Hank killed his wife and left Tommy as little more than a vegetable, there's no use pretending it didn't happen, it did, and both of them got what they deserved, but God can forgive him that so why can't a simple town cop? Hank didn't poison innocent kids or butcher women or send thousands to the gas chambers, or a hundred other shitty things men have done to each other down through history and will do again. Forgiveness goes hand in glove with acceptance, is what I'm saying.

That doesn't stop me from doing my job.

When he finished drinking, I told Hank, "There's going to be questions. In no time at all the town will be overrun with reporters and lawyers and cops. Hot-shot cops from the RCMP, guys who don't know you like I do."

"I wanted the baby," he said. "And that was a mistake."

I thought oh God, Hank, don't turn into a basket case. Don't do that to yourself. To me. "Hank," I said, level but firm, "I'll do what I can."

"It was Tommy," he said. "She wouldn't listen."

"Try to protect you."

"It was Tommy," he repeated.

Nothing I said was getting through to him. "Okay, Hank," I said. I put one hand on his elbow, real firm. "Let's go now."

"She didn't have to. You understand? Dix?"

We stopped on the way to the station house so Hank could puke in the ditch. "Sorry," he said to me as we climbed back up the dew-slippery grass. "For putting you through all this – this blood and what not." His eyes were still glassy but they were not flickering about as they had been.

I'd seen a lot worse. In Korea we'd left our dig-in early one morning on a recon and come across a family that had been butchered by the side of the road. Bodies mutilated, limbs tossed on the ground. You don't get used to that even when it becomes familiar. We saw something new that morning. Two kids, boys of eight or ten, it was hard to tell, alive but huddled in some bushes not far off. Brothers, cousins. Their ears had been cut off. Just that. Ears hacked away like the heads off fishes. They had their hands cupped over their heads where their ears had been, I reckon they were cold and sore, and blood dribbled from between their fingers and ran down their necks. They stood awkwardly when we dragged them from the bushes. They were crying. One of my men asked, "Should we shoot them, sarge, put them out of their misery?" He held his rifle across his chest at the ready. "Jesus," I said, "we're not animals." I knew as I said it how wrong that was. We were animals – are – and I learned it anew every day over there. How else do you explain cutting the ears off innocent kids? Like I say, there's lots worse than Hank Peterson.

At the station house Billy Jewett was getting ready to pick up Butch Russell, who had stabbed Cecil Werner when he'd arrived home from the Rockland around dawn. Butch had been laying for him. They both lived in that part of town near the curling rink where the houses were little more than tar-paper shacks and nobody had the right to stand on their pride, but neither would back down if the other pulled a blade. Knife fights. I don't know why miners like them. Personally it was the one thing I hated about commando training, sneaking up behind a man and slitting his throat. Give me a good clean fire fight any day. Even a punch out. Some guys were good with knives, the same guys, it turned out, who cheated at cards and beat their women. Miners carry these hunting knives strapped to their belts, like a six-gun, only you can't carry a six-gun in this country. Which is the point.

Anyways, back in those days the guy working midnight to 8:00 had to disarm some drunken bastard with a knife every now and then. Usually down the far end of a dark alley or somewheres else where there's no room to dodge. I hate that. You cannot go in there unarmed, but you can't go after some knife-wielding drunk with a pistol either. You shoot the bastard, which is what he's got coming, and there's no end of hand-wringing and weeping and wailing from the town council and Mike Leachman and anyone else who reckons they have an opinion on police conduct. None of whom ever has gone down a back alley at night, never mind one with a Butch Russell waiting at the end of it. The way to do it is this: bicycle chain in one hand, baseball bat in the other. You can usually disable the knife hand by wrapping the chain around the arm. Then a few clean licks with the bat – knees and ribs if you can get at them – it's all over. One thing about a dark alley: you feel like laying on a few extra licks, there's nobody around to stop you.

Butch Russell was not an easy man to take. Built like a fire hydrant and mean as a junkyard dog to boot. He and his shit-for-brains brothers had hired on as company scabs when the union guys blocked the road to the mines that August. I'll never understand that, men with so little self-respect they'll take the job of a guy who has a beef with his bosses. The way I figure it, stay out of a man's business and he'll stay out of yours. We all need to keep a little dignity about two things, our jobs and our wives, the others don't matter. Make things easy, is my motto. So one of the first things I tell the guys who work for me is, "Keep your nose clean." Otherwise it's like you're pushing in between a man and his wife when they've got stuff to work out between them. Their business. But guys like the Russells, they're so busy showing the world nobody pushes them around, they've got no time for the other guy. A mining town has more than its fair share of that type.

Not that I have any time for unions either. Behind all their talk the union guys are just clawing to get whatever they can, the old snatch and grab. Their leaders are worse, if you ask me – which nobody is. I'm talking about the bigwigs who swish into Red Rock every year or so in their black Cadillacs to make sure the local boys vote them in again. Loco boys, is more like it. These guys in top coats from Montréal, some place they scuttle right back to, they're not spending an extra night at the Rockland or eating more breakfasts at The Steep Rock Café than they can possibly help. The set-up, is this: the town cop gets to stand outside the door where the vote is going on with the pug types the bigwigs hire to drive their Caddys and throw around a little muscle when it's needed. They call that union politics. I've had the pleasure of shaking the bigwigs' hands, too. Guys with diamond rings on their pinkies, guys who smell better than women. Like I say, nothing more than the old snatch and grab, only a little more out in the open than usual.

About Butch Russell. On the mine road that August Cecil Werner had got into a scrap with Butch's brother Terry and busted his nose. Deserved it, no doubt. That was before Max and me pulled up in the squad car. It was the usual striker-scab business, one row of vehicles, the strikers, strung across the road and two or three pickups of scabs trying to break across it. One thing about a mining town: there's always lots of action. The strikers had pickets and were waving them in the faces of the scabs, who had baseball bats. There was a lot of pushing and shoving and a few punches, as I said, and later I heard both sides had guns in their vehicles. Wading through that mob, I had one fist clenched and my other hand on the butt of my service revolver. You never know. Guys were screaming in our faces but I just kept saying, "All right now, boys, let's all just settle down."

We made the peace, Max and me, standing between the two bands and letting them shout themselves out. That's the way you handle these strike confrontations. Try keep the lid on while the anger runs itself down. Like hauling in a pike you got on your line too big for the weight test. Patience. You try not to take sides. You try to minimize the physical aspect, which is tough because you're taking all this verbal abuse and shit and what you'd really like to do is give a couple of these loud mouth bastards a poke in the mouth. Most of them would back down like dogs, believe me, a man with any salt calls their bluff.

But you got to take it lying down. That time I'm referring to here, Max got a crack on the back of the head and I got spat on for our trouble. At least it wasn't a knife in the back, which is what you can expect from those bastards most times.

That happened here. At one time I hired constables from the town, reckoning being from Red Rock the miners would cut a local boy a little slack and vice versa. This kid Dave Lee had been out of school a couple years, worked at the mine, that sort of thing, and he wanted to get into the Mounties so he thought he'd get a taste of being a cop by working for the town. He was a likable kid, and big. Stood six-two and weighed a good two-thirty. Nothing wrong with a little beef when you're a cop. He had thin blond hair stood up on his head and one of those wide open faces that invites teasing in school, a good-looking kid. Dave was just getting the hang of the job when along comes one of these strikes, we get them every year or two, there's nothing for it but take them as they come, like the snow storms in winter. The worst are the wildcats, which this was.

We'd driven out to the mine road, parked the squad car and waded into the mob. I like my men to keep close together in these confrontations, back each other up, like, but this mob was huge, surging back and forth, shoving, yelling, screaming abuse from all sides. The strike had being going on for weeks and tempers were flaring. During a wildcat you've got the men with the union fighting the men against the union and both of them fighting the scabs.

One-hundred-per-cent cock-up. Already two or three men had been stabbed, so the whole town was on edge. On top of that, it was a hot day, middle of summer. Everyone seemed to have a red face. You could smell the anger. I wished I'd known there were so many men on the mine road before we'd left because I'd have called in Max and the RCMP guys from the Lakehead. I take pride in knowing when it's my cue to fight, but I missed the boat that day.

I told Dave the usual: "Just keep at them to calm down. Calm down, got it?" We cut past the pickups blocked by the cars and that's where we got separated, at the axis of the two sets of vehicles. That bothered me right off. He was a big kid, and capable of handling himself one on one, but Dave knew zilch about crowds. The noise, the fact you're surrounded by hundreds of angry men, the threat of physical violence, all have a way of unnerving cops who have been on the job for years. You can feel this pressure building. It's frightening, the first few times. You start backing away when the only way to deal with a crowd is to push forward. And the heat that day was something else. It was a furnace at the centre of those men.

I'd told Dave what I tell every cop going in: do not touch anyone, whatever the provocation. That's the way to turn a showdown into a riot. Dave was taking me literally. The last I saw of him he had his arms up in the air over the miners' heads. It was almost comical. Then I got spun around by the movement of the crowd. Someone was in my face, one of the Russells or the Werners, yelling stuff about the assholes running the mines and how I was protecting the sons of bitches by breaking up a legal action. Which, being a wildcat strike, it wasn't. "I've got a cap in my hand," he shouted, meaning dynamite, "for the bosses, and a blade for you, Dixon – if you're man enough to try me. You man enough? Or you going to hide behind your tin badge? You only good for sucking the cocks of company bosses?"

You can see how easy it is to lose your head in one of these situations.

By the time I'd worked my way round the bastard Dave had disappeared from sight, but a circle had formed down the line of strikers' cars and I knew from the way it was moving something bad had happened. I clawed through the mob, losing my hat in the process. When they saw me coming the men gave way. I saw Hank there, and Stan Spelchak, too. There was still lots of yelling, threats and accusations, mostly. I felt a picket strike my shin and later had a lump there for a month. Dave was on both knees, hunched forward. When he raised his head I saw a patch of blood on his blue shirt. Some son of a bitch had stabbed him. The blade went in just below the rib cage. I reached down, tore his shirt open and put my hand inside. Dave looked at me like a dog that doesn't know why it's been kicked. "My hands," he whispered, "I kept them in the air." The big dumb ox was apologizing. It made your heart ache. He tried to raise his arms to show me, but the pain of moving stopped him and he lurched forward. I caught him in my arms. I felt the hole where the flesh had been pierced by the knife. You wouldn't have thought a little wound like that could kill a man.

I'd seen lots of men die in Korea, ugly deaths, but this was different. Back in '52 I was a kid fighting alongside other kids, and we expected to die. When one of us went over it was tough, but we'd set our teeth to it, to dying and seeing each other die. If we reacted, it was by drinking ourselves numb that night or going out the next day and charging a machine gun nest on top of a hill. There was no feeling there except ice cold rage. But this was not like that. Dave was like a son to me, a big innocent boy who just ended up dead one day. He'd likely never even had a piece of tail. He hardly bled at all.

What I mean is, we see a lot of death in these granite hills, not counting the shootings and knifings and car pile-ups at Dead Man's Curve. Drownings in the lakes and rivers. Domestic death, call it. And then every couple years one of these multiple murders, a guy finds his wife cheating on him and lays them both out in a pool of blood. Becky and Tommy were not the first.

Once we'd taken Hank's fingerprints and locked him in the tank I had to go back to the house. The Coroner, Doc McCabe, would want to look around, for one. Also the ambulance guys would be returning for Becky's body, and I needed to make notes on the scene and so on. I phoned Alice first, telling her I'd be on the job twelve or sixteen hours, which she already knew, seeing as how the whole hospital was buzzing about Tommy and Becky and Hank. Word had it Hank had been booking off work early for a couple weeks, waiting for his opportunity. I didn't believe that for a minute but made a mental note to check it out. I told Alice I'd have to stay in town all weekend. The reporters would be flooding in, the lawyers, the RCMP. We'd been planning a supper at the Flame Club and I didn't want her to conclude it had been ruined. Women put a lot of store by these things.

I called Max and told him we'd all have to work overtime, which pleased him no end, let me tell you. I was betting the town's budget committee were not going to be happy either. But what can you do? I didn't make folks the way they are, I just try to clean up after. That second time I took my notebook to the Petersons'.

When I got there Doc McCabe and Mike Leachman from the *Record* were sitting on the steps, waiting. They stood as I approached.

"Morning, Dixon," Mike said.

I reflexively glanced at the sky: same grey clouds, like mattress stuffing, as earlier, not a *good* morning at all. I asked the doc, "How's Tommy?"

"Holding steady."

"Meaning?"

"Meaning he's going to live. Most likely. Meaning, it's going to be a long haul. He may have to be moved to Winnipeg on a moment's notice. Meaning, before you get your hopes up, nobody can even think of talking to him for at least a week."

"Jesus, Joseph, and Mary."

"He's unconscious. Right out. Worse, one lung is virtually gone and the other barely functioning. The blast got him in the middle of the back. There must be a thousand pellets in him I'll have to dig out once he's stable."

"You save them. They're evidence."

We had moved to the top of the steps and I was unlocking the door, one of those new-fangled brass jobs. Mike said, "Are you letting me in Dixon?"

"I can't stop you," I said. "But don't touch anything. Not one thing."

We walked down the hall. We stood in the doorway, all three of us cramped like sardines, and studied the room. The smell was awful. "I think," Doc McCabe said, "I'll open a window in here."

The bed sat in the middle of the room, with space to pass along it on each side. The window Doc McCabe had in mind was on the side of the bed where Tommy had fallen, to our right. "Don't smudge up that chalk," I said. I'd had just enough time earlier to do a quick outline of the bodies and wanted to go over them again.

The doc hesitated for a second.

Mike was looking at the bed. "It's odd," he said, "what you learn about people from their bedrooms. Those are linen sheets. I don't think we've ever had anything but cotton on ours. Flannelette in winter."

The doc said, "Me and Hildi slept on satin once in Chicago."

We stood for a moment at the foot of the bed in silence, looking at Becky's sheet-draped body. No matter how often you've seen a dead body there's still that moment when you don't know what else to do. Mike coughed and cleared his throat.

The doc said, "You figure he shot them both from here?" He pointed to the corner where Tommy had lain and then to the bed where we'd found Becky.

"Right. First one, then the other. Wham, wham."

"That makes sense," the doc said. "The position of the bodies and all." He nodded his head. He'd stepped over toward the window and was fingering the curtains absent-mindedly. He fumbled with the catches on the window. When it opened he sighed, "That's better."

We looked at each other.

"Yeah," Mike said. "You don't really notice until the fresh air hits you."

"It's cold," I said. "It better not mess up the evidence."

The doc said, "This is odd." He pulled the curtain out gingerly, between his thumb and forefinger. "There's a hand print here. A couple, actually."

He was right. When he pulled the curtain material taut, flattening the folds out completely, we could make out the clear outline of hand prints, two of them, in iron red, smudged, but hand prints all the same.

Mike asked, "How did those get there?"

"Somebody grabbed the curtain," the doc said.

"When I first saw Hank this morning," I said, "his hands were filthy, like he'd come straight from the pits without washing up. Could have been him."

Mike said, "It shows how worked up Hank was. How upset."

"It's two hands, right?" the doc said. He looked from me to Mike and then back again. "Right?"

"Right," I said.

The doc studied the prints on the curtain, holding the white material up to the light coming in at the window. He said, "That means…." He looked out the window.

"It means it was Hank grabbed the curtain," I said.

"With both hands," the doc said. "See." He gestured with the curtain.

"Probably he slipped," Mike said, "coming round the end of the bed. Didn't Roy say there was vomit on the floor? And urine?"

"If he grabbed the curtain with both hands," the doc said, "then where was the gun?"

"He put it down."

"But you said Roy took the gun from him when he came into the house."

"That's right," I said. "Hank put the shotgun down, then he picked the shotgun up again. So what?"

"I don't know," the doc said. "But it might mean something."

Mike said, "Hummm."

"Shit," I said. "You know how I hate this Sherlock Holmes stuff. Blood stains here, a lock of hair there. Come on, doc, this is as simple as it gets. The guy came home and found his wife with another man and he did what any red-blooded man would do. He taught the bastard and the bitch a lesson. Bam, bam. End of story."

Mike said, "I won't quote you on that."

"No," I said, "you bloody well better not."

"Still," the doc said. He looked from the bed where Becky's body had been to the stains on the floor where Tommy had lain and then at Becky's sheet-covered body. He took a polka-dotted handkerchief out of his back pocket and blew his nose in it loudly. I sensed even then that he was not going to be my best witness, and truth be told the doc's confusing testimony at the trial delayed the inevitable and nearly got Hank hung, though that was exactly the opposite of what the doc intended when he launched into his cock-eyed nonsense about Becky shooting herself.

"Come on," I said, "let's get this over with."

The doc got out his note pad and ball point. I got out my chalk and kneeled on the floor to re-draw Tommy's outline. The smell down there made me gag. "Look here," I said to the doc.

He stooped beside me and examined a bloody lump about the size of a walnut. "Cloth," he said. "Most likely cloth from Tommy's clothing clotted with flesh and blood on impact. There may be a pellet of buckshot in there." I held it gingerly between thumb and forefinger and deposited it in an envelope I'd brought for collecting evidence.

We stood. Mike was looking at the sheet over

Becky's body. I pinched a corner of it between two fingers and lifted slowly. What a fine young piece gone to waste. Not exactly the words I'd use in describing her to Alice.

"God," the doc said, "half her face is gone."

Mike looked away and coughed.

I leaned over and closed the one eye that was left. Funny, I'd always thought Becky had the blue eyes. It was Hank. Shows you can be wrong.

"He'd have to have been right on top of her to do that kind of damage," the doc said. "Right on top of her." He moved back and studied her from an angle, already formulating the theory that confused the jury and made the judge troop us all through the crime scene in the middle of the trial.

I said, "It was one barrel each. Tommy first, it looks, then her."

Mike said, "I wonder if they said anything. Yelled or screamed."

"It doesn't make sense," the doc said.

"You'd think somebody might have heard. Roy or Lyle, maybe."

"Tommy, now, from the size of the wound, the density of the buckshot, yes, that shot had to be fired from just inside the room. The doorway, or near the doorway. But this. You do not walk right up to somebody's face with a shotgun and then pull the trigger."

"The woman you love," said Mike.

"Yeah," I said. "Whatever that has to do with anything."

Mike waved his hand in the air, palm flipped up,

protesting. "Dixon," he said. He sounded like Lyle, and I wondered if they were girl friends.

"You done?" I asked. The doc was rubbing the end of his chin with one finger, contemplating the hand prints on the curtains or something. I wish I'd known where his thoughts were heading. I could have saved us all a lot of embarrassment and the state a pile of money.

"Can I take a picture?" Mike asked. "Of the room," he added.

It was an open-and-shut case but the Crown prosecutors love to have pictures in the file. "All right," I said. "And a couple of Becky, too, but not for publication." It was an arrangement that had worked out in the past. Mike got his photos for the *Record,* not-too-sensational shots of the scene, and I got mine for the evidence files. When Mike was finished, I pulled the sheet back over the body. So much for Becky Peterson, one-time prom queen.

The doc scribbled something in his note pad. "Don't get it," he said.

"What's to understand? A man comes home, finds his bride in bed with another man and that's that."

"That's just it," Mike said. "His bride, the woman he loves, mother of his kid. That's what doesn't add up."

"Jesus," I said. We had moved away from the body. I had to re-do the chalk outline on the bed. "It's a question of honour, is what I'm saying."

"I don't know," the doc said. "Tommy I can understand."

"What I'm saying is, there comes a time when a

man knows it's not a question of what's right or wrong in society's eyes, he's not concerned about that any longer. He's taken a certain amount of shit and he's come to the point where his mind is set on one thing and that alone. The only thing that matters is how he feels right here. In his gut."

"Maybe so," Mike said, "some men."

"He has to live there, inside his own skin. Him, and no one else." I stood up from where I'd been leaning over the bed. "It's like a fist fight. You don't fight unless it's a matter of losing honour, but once you're in it, you're in it."

"That's a mighty dark view of life," Mike said.

"It's the way it is." I put the chalk back into my pocket. "That's it for me," I said, nodding at the doc. "You?"

Doc said, "I guess the shells stayed in the chamber."

"Honour," I said. "It's not logical, it's not right even. But it makes sense."

Doc put his hand on my elbow. "Where is the gun, by the way?"

I said, "I've got it in the trunk. Nice and safe."

"Good," the doc said.

"Locked away nice and safe."

"Good," Mike said. "And thanks, Dixon."

I walked them to the door and watched them drive off. Men like Mike, college men, don't understand how the real world works – they are always looking for explanations and excuses when it's usually the simple things drive folks to do what they do – greed and lust and anger. A man takes what's yours – your wife – and you kill him. If he doesn't get you first.

Back inside I looked around the bedroom again. There were pictures on the walls, a winter scene and a summer. I'd helped Hank move the bed from Eaton's one Saturday afternoon a couple years earlier. When we'd put up the rails and thrown the mattress in place he'd bounced on it and joked about the springs. "Lots of bounce," he said, laughing. He told me Becky made him sleep on the living-room couch when he came home late from the bar after MineKings games. *You stink,* he'd said, imitating her voice, and *Stop groping me.* Hank thought that was really funny. The Dragon Lady, he'd called Becky. Around the dressing room he'd say, *I haven't had a piece of tail in years. The closest I get is that pair of rubber boots in the shed.*

A good-looking broad like Becky, it was all talk, we thought. Shit.

The thing is you just never know. The guy who brags about how he always gets lucky, he's likely whacking off in the bathroom. The guy who jokes about not getting it in years likely hasn't. It's a fucked-up world.

Becky, now, there was talk around town that Tommy wasn't the first guy she took on while married to Hank. Nurses, they have a reputation for being easy. You're looking for a horny bunch, there's your ticket. It must be seeing death every day makes you appreciate what life has to offer. It's the same with funerals. You ever notice the two things happen when you get home from a funeral? You can't stop eating and you're as horny as a two-peckered owl. The life urges rising up.

Everybody knows about how Becky carried on in high school. There was that Irish construction crew guy when she was what, in Grade Ten. He had long side-burns and wore yellow leather gloves on the job. You saw Becky and him in The Steep Rock Café for a couple weeks and then one afternoon I stumble across his car on that side road just before the Crystal Lake turn off, windows steamed up. I did not investigate. I figure why bring Sam Johnson down on my head in a statutory rape case. Then one Saturday night a year or so later I'm walking the beat downtown and I see Becky with two Indians, Joey Armstead and his brother, Johnny. They were in their twenties, worked at the lumber mill at Sapawe owned by their cousin, and Becky was in Grade Twelve, a girl with a skinny little body and a tinkly laugh, likely still kept dolls on her bed. Jesus, Joseph, and Mary, I says to myself. Those Armsteads are nice enough guys when sober but they play hockey like it's Custer's Last Stand and the fact is you never see them when they're not half drunk. I've hardly taken that information in when I spot Sam Johnson, strolling down Main Street about two blocks behind them, but keeping to the shadows.

Then a week later Alice tells me over supper that

one night Sam brought Becky into the General with bruises all over her legs. When was this? I ask her. Why didn't I hear about it? I'm reckoning right away those goddamned bucks took her out to some gravel pit and beat her when she wouldn't come across. I'm halfway out of my chair, thinking of paying a surprise visit out Sapawe way, when Alice puts her hand on my arm. "Listen, Dixon," she says, dropping her eyes to her plate, "don't go flying off half-cocked before you've heard what I have to say. Sam wanted the hospital to keep it hush-hush. Not a word, he says to the girls on duty, letting them see in those steel grey eyes he means business. You know Sam Johnson."

I have to chew that over for a while. What I'm saying is, there was talk when Becky was just a kid that Christine Johnson packed up and went back to wherever they come from, Boston was it, because Sam was beating the girl. A neighbour had seen him in the window one night, belt raised over his head and the kid lying on the floor, shielding herself with her hands, Christine between, screaming at him to stop. Becky had been into the hospital once or twice before that with suspicious bruises on her legs, falling down stairs, the official story. There was talk around the school, too. In a small town, things come out. That was all over, Christine had told some of the women at the church when she came back from the east. She'd told Sam that he raised his hand to the girl again, she'd be gone, and the next he'd hear from her would be by way of a lawyer. All that gives me something to chew over. I'm saying you take a girl acts like

Becky did in high school there has to be a reason – it's not just she was born that way.

By that time I was sitting on the bed. At my feet was Becky's body, the sheet over top. Any minute the ambulance guys were going to come back and take it away. I thought to myself I've got a report to type out, and the image of myself sitting at the ancient Smith-Corona in the office when I could have been home between cool sheets made me more tired than I'd felt since dawn, when I'd been eyeing the clock waiting for shift's end. I found myself patting my pockets for tobacco, a habit I'd given up when I started sleeping over at Alice's.

That was a couple of years after I moved to Red Rock. We met at a town picnic where I was dishing out ice cream, part of the human relations aspect of the job, let the kids see the cop's just an ordinary guy like dad, and Alice was serving coffee at the next table. We'd seen each other from a distance before, but nothing had come of it. Then in the middle of this picnic she walks by me with an urn of coffee and I give her a little pat on the ass. She pretended she didn't notice, set the urn down on a table, and went on pouring coffee. Half an hour later I'm bent over the ice cream barrel digging the hard stuff at the bottom when I feel a hand close over my balls. Real tight. It takes my breath away. "You try that again, buster," she whispers in a voice I'm not sure is meant to be a real warning or playful, "and I'll have the law on you so fast it'll make your head spin."

We dated for a while, drove to the Lakehead for

weekends, and I started staying over at her place nights, and then we got married. I got no complaints in that department, never have.

Neither of us is from Red Rock, and we weren't planning on growing old here, but it has its attractions. For me, hunting and fishing, besides playing hockey, a game I'd starred at as an underage junior before dropping out of school in Medicine Hat, a town in the foothills of Alberta where we'd never heard of hematite or Euclids, even if my father, an insurance agent, had nothing good to say about unions and said it all the time. I left there at eighteen and joined the Army. Alice came from Fort Frances, a pulp and paper town two hours to the west of Red Rock by train, also a union town. She finished high school, did her RN in Winnipeg, and moved to Red Rock when a doctor she thought she was in love with turned out to be the bastard all her friends had been warning her he was.

When I moved here Red Rock had the reputation of being a tough town. It still does in some quarters. But we've cleaned it up considerable, me and my constables, over the years. When I got here it was common practice for miners to buy a two-four of beer and sit on the curb side with their buddies, jeering at passing cars and God knows what all else. Assaulting women, pissing in the bushes. I put a stop to it. That's how my nose got busted the first time. If I was to do it today, I'd pick someone other than Barry Werner to make a point with. At the time I didn't know better, and it worked in my favour. I acquired an instant reputation for not taking shit. Arnold Piper told me about a month after I took the job, "You don't pick your spots, do you Dixon?" And he was right. In the Army the boxing coach said I was fast and tough but had the bad habit of leading with my chin. What I mean is, you're a fighter, you earn a little respect in a town like this. We got the assault rate down to the national average, we got the drunk driving to where the idiots only kill themselves most of the time, we've even curbed the statutory rape. The one that really bugs my butt is murder.

Murder's a crime you can't control, is what I'm saying. Those others, you let the town know you won't stand for public indecency, you put up a show of force when you need to, just to make a point, get your nose busted showing you mean business, slap a few dead beats around on Saturday night, wave your pistol in some faces, in less time than you reckon a town shapes up, even starts to take pride in itself. You begin to hear folks talking about the fun they had at a dance, not who punched out who. Girls can walk the street after supper without getting pawed, kids don't have to witness a knife fight out front of The Steep Rock Café on their way home from school on pay day. A little ordinary decency comes back into daily life. Murder, however. Just when you got the town humming like a well-oiled machine and you're half-beginning to believe the Mayor's claim that you're the best thing to happen to the town, bango, some idiot takes a gun to his wife and the newspapers from Vancouver to St. John's are calling your town the sin capital of the nation.

In my books nine times out of ten murder is not premeditated. If it were, I'd be the happiest man in the country. What I'm saying is, then I could control it and hold a lid on it. Most murders I've seen, somebody – some guy – goes off his rocker. That's all there is to it. There is no way to anticipate it, no way to head it off. That's the shits of it from the law enforcement side of things – even if you hear lawyers arguing all the time, premeditated this and that. The other thing they're always on about is deterrence. Hand out a stiff sentence, the judges are told, that will work as deterrence. In a pig's ear, is what I say. Not a single murder in Red Rock these past thirty years would have been prevented because the sentence was hanging, or electric chair, or chopping guys' dicks off with the guillotine in the town square at high noon, for that matter. Don't get me wrong. I'm all in favour of teaching the bastards a lesson who rape and murder and so on. An eye for an eye. But don't confuse that with preventing the next guy from committing violent crime. You can deter your break-and-entry types with the paddle and whippings, they're busting into citizens' homes rather than making a decent living, but that's the extent of it. Your murderer is just not going to be stopped by abstract things like the possibility of a stiff sentence. A pistol in the face, yes.

Not that I don't reckon premeditated murder doesn't occur. It does. When I was in basic training I had this corporal, Henderson. He was a bull of a man and mean as a pig when crossed. He found out his wife was cheating on him with some guy from the city and he worked out a plan. "Dixon," he told me one night when we were having a few beers, "Dixon, I'm going to kill that bastard and that little minx and then I'm going to get away with it by claiming temporary insanity." Sure, sure, I thinks. Just another guy blowing off steam. Have another beer.

Next time he's on furlough Henderson takes a cab to his own address, walks up the front steps, turns the key in the door, and grabs this guy right out of the bed where he and the little wife are at it. He doesn't hit him, he doesn't even say anything to him. He grabs him in a bear hug and squeezes him to death. Can you beat that? He was big, like I say, arms the size of hams. Just crushed that poor bastard's lungs by wrapping his arms round him, suffocated him, his wife standing right there in her nightie or whatever. After he's sure the guy's dead, he drops him to the floor, then walks around looking dazed, saying *Where am I ? What have I done?* pulling his hair, so when the cops get there they put him down as crazy and stick him into a straightjacket. In court his lawyer argues Henderson stumbled into the house unaware of what was going on, lost his mind when he saw what was happening, and did the first thing came to him, which was grab the other guy. If he was premeditating murder, his lawyer says, a man wouldn't take a taxi cab and draw attention to his movements, he would go to the house armed with a weapon, and so on. His lawyer argues Henderson didn't intend to kill the guy at all, just grabbed him out of instinct – and the next thing you know the guy's lungs are crushed. His lawyer asks the jury to look at Henderson. He asks them *Do you believe this man cold-bloodedly planned to hug a man so hard he'd kill him?* There's a titter in the courtroom over that. The jury lets him off scot-free.

Back in the barracks he says to me, "I told you, Dixon, I'd kill that s.o.b. and get away with it. All you need is a plan, all you need is to be smarter than they think you are." We bought each other beers at the enlisted men's bar and felt pretty smug about how clever he'd been. Even fooled his lawyer. 'Course that's not the end of the story. His very next furlough Henderson goes through the same routine with his wife, only this time the jury gets wise and sends him to the chair. Like I say, mistakes. He got away with it once, but folks don't like you making fools of them.

With Hank the situation was entirely different. He sat there throughout the trial, looking blank and confused and yet somehow completely at peace with himself. The prosecuting attorneys had all the evidence in their favour – the shotgun, the booking off early from work, the witnesses – and they went after them like dogs to a pork chop. They had fingerprints and blood samples, thanks to me. They had photographs. They had statements from dozens of folks. They argued Hank thought the whole thing through. They demonstrated motive, intent, opportunity, and forethought, and they drew a touching picture of Becky and would have dragged the hapless Tommy into the courtroom for the jury to see the visible evidence of Hank's murderous rampage if Tommy hadn't been flat on his back in a coma. They played on the plight of young Scott. I was convinced, but it didn't work with the jury. They felt sorry for Hank despite the fact he was clearly guilty. He hadn't even gone to the trouble of storing the gun in the hall closet or going into work shit-face drunk so the foreman at the pits had to send him home early. He was an idiot, but such an obvious one the jury decided Hank was the injured party and Becky deserved what she got, so they called it temporary insanity. If it was me I would have argued justifiable homicide. *Insanity* demeans a man, in my opinion. But my opinion didn't count for much.

No one asked in any case. They did want to know about the locations of things and the sequence of events and other details of evidence. I was glad to provide them, though I left out the bits about the blood looking like pigs' guts and the smell worse than an outhouse. I stuck to the facts, then and now, that's a cop's duty and I always do mine. I got no time for opinions and theories and looking back with regret. All that does is leave you open to the scorn of the folks who are supposed to respect you and the law you represent. You offer an opinion on the stand and some lawyer twists it around and suddenly you're the laughing stock of the whole town. I've seen that happen. One little slip and all the work you've done to make a town a decent place to live in can unravel faster than a bad sock. Listen, I know what folks around Red Rock think of me, how they spit on the town cop one minute and come running for him to hold their hand the next. Like I say, this job.

The Stranger Within

Manson Welch:

This is not a story I'm particularly happy to tell, since it reflects so badly on me, or on who I once was, back in the days when I could be numbered among journalism's hot shots, a dubious distinction I know now, but one I was proud of at the time.

When Nate at the *Weekend* called I had already packed my bag. It was noon that Friday and the early radio reports were coming in: wife and lover shot by husband. It was too good to be true. And in a mining town, yet, a crucible of vice if God ever designed one: transients and toughs, jealousy and lust. I'd witnessed it before, while covering the asbestos strikes in Québec and had knocked out some of my best pieces for the *Weekend*. So, yes, I was packed and ready to go as soon as he said, "Manny, this one's for you." I'd even taken the old Ford to the garage for an oil change because I knew I could outrun the CNR and beat the kids from the dailies to the scene.

Sometimes they can make this job harder than it already is, what with grieving parents and distraught wives and the rest of the agony that goes along with human pain. Those kids are always trampling around on people's feelings while they try to get their stories, and the problem is if they get to mucking about before you do, you have a hard time getting anything out of your key witnesses. People become suspicious of reporters quickly and clam up and you lose your story. You have to get them while their passions are smouldering.

I am not a sensationalist. And I do not think the worst of my neighbour. But I know that every person I've ever come across is driven by passions. Yes, we're all just boiling up inside. I don't know why, I don't pretend to, I leave that to Dr. Freud and his crowd. But I see it every time I get into a story: the pain, the grief, the anger of just being alive on this planet. That's why I have to laugh when the neighbours of the Boston Strangler or whoever say they don't get it, he seemed such a quiet guy. They don't get it is right. Behind all our calm faces there's demons burning us up. I'm not just talking about the guys who chop up girls and bury them in the back yard. I'm talking about ordinary lust and madness: kids with knives, fathers who go berserk, Rocket Richard, for pete's sake, busting his stick over Hal Laycoe's head. The more calm on the outside, you might say, the more lust and fury on the inside. The odd thing is people are too stupid to grasp the idea or refuse to accept it. When I was a hot shot I thought my job was to keep pointing it out.

One thing I can say for certain, the drive up was spectacular. I'm not the type to go ga-ga over trees and lakes. Mother, now, she can talk about flowers for hours. Knows the names of birds, too. When she starts in on something as simple as the warbler she can talk the ear off the elephant. I've never seen the point. Birds squawk in the mornings and shit on the lawn furniture every time you turn around, so what's the fuss? Get me past robins and blue jays, I'm in trouble. I'm not even sure the flock that picks at the gravel in the driveway is sparrows – and I don't understand why you'd care to know.

The country near Red Rock is nothing but lakes and trees. And rocks. They've had to cut the highway through the Shield, blasting first, it appears, to break up these huge monoliths of granite and then slice away at it to make a space wide enough for two lanes of blacktop. And not for a measly twenty miles or something. Whoever did this must have been at it for years, hacking through rock from Sudbury to the prairies. When you whiz by in your car at sixty miles an hour it doesn't seem much, but it's awe-inspiring if you see it up close. Past Lake Superior I got out of the car to stretch my legs. I'd been driving for hours and needed air. I climbed up one of those granite hills. The sun was just rising in front of me, coming over the tops of the scrub spruces in a haze of gold. Mist floated up from the swampy ground, *muskeg* they call it in Red Rock, and black birds were cackling in a stand of bulrushes growing in the ditch, dozens of them. I stood with my hands in my pockets and listened. Frogs called out, and deep in the dense bush I heard crashing, a tree falling, or a moose in the underbrush. It was eerie. Not another human soul for miles. I'd passed a milk truck half an hour earlier but hadn't seen a car for two hours.

There was nothing up there but miles and miles of bush. Perhaps ten million acres of scrub spruce and jack pine and stands of poplar and thousands of lakes you can spit across. There were mosquitoes, though, and swarms of dragonflies that lift off the water into your face. The people huddle in towns dotted along the highway, a Husky station here, a general store with a tin sign out front there, tiny outposts of civilization in an expanse of nature that's next to never-ending. Not the kind of territory you want to be driving through. Yet it was thrilling as well as frightening.

I'm from Toronto so I have a city boy's notion of what *park* means: a cheery grassy area you can walk across in twenty minutes. When I learned later that I was standing that morning in something called Quetico Provincial Park I laughed aloud. That park is bigger than the province of Nova Scotia. If an airplane came down in there, you'd have trouble walking out in three weeks, provided you survived the mosquitoes.

And yet I liked it. There was something wild about the country that touched the wild part in me, my primitive side. That may sound corny. But out there you felt the same way you feel standing beside the ocean listening to the waves crashing in. It seems someone is trying to warn you about something. In Red Rock you heard it in the wind. At night you stood outside and looked up at towering pines that rattled like they were speaking. The Arctic wind blowing down from Hudson Bay rushed through those woods and a thrill swept up your spine. Stand there long enough and you heard scuffling in the undergrowth, then sudden silence, a primitive kill going down in the primeval darkness. I understood why people felt edgy there. How things could get out of hand.

Most of the towns I'd driven through on the way around Lake Superior were only shacks clustered at the side of the road. You knew the kinds of lives lived there by the look of the houses – flapping tar-paper on the roofs, plastic covering the windows, rusty junk heaps out front. I caught a glimpse of the children from time to time: torn jeans, dirty faces, scrawny necks and arms. Those kids are poor. In Cabbagetown you see people trapped by poverty and wonder how they keep their dignity. On the road to Red Rock you wonder how they stay alive. What is there to do in the middle of nowhere? Fish, hunt, scrounge in the bush for berries and whatnot, like the first settlers to this land? There isn't even a tourist trade to enslave the locals as fishing guides and car mechanics and waitresses.

Red Rock was a surprise. From the time you leave Port Arthur you've been travelling through muskeg country for over an hour. Then you come through the granite hills around several sharp bends and into a sudden valley with a clear river running through it. There's an older section of town with decaying buildings, but once you cross the tracks, the houses become quite spiffy. In the downtown sector the streets were paved, the buildings single-storey frame and stucco, fresh paint, white walls. It was not a pulp and paper town where every exposed surface gets covered with effluence from belching smokestacks, or a smelter town where the windows of stores are coated with oily grime. At one time Red Rock was prosperous. You could tell that from the cars on the streets, most of them the sharper models, Meteors and Belairs, and so on. The high school sat on the ring road, a sprawling brick building with a freshly-sodded football field and white goal posts. On the far side of town the hospital, same red brick with a paved parking lot.

I circled the town and drove up and down Main Street a couple of times before going into The Steep Rock Café for breakfast. It was just past seven on a Saturday morning, but the booths were full and I had to take a seat at the counter. Sausage and poached eggs on toast (soggy) served by a friendly woman named Irene who recommended the hotel downtown where the lawyers were booked in, reason enough for me to try the Rockton Motel just off the ring road.

The train from Toronto was due in two hours and I knew the kids would be climbing all over the scene once they arrived, but I had a two-hour lead, so I changed shirts, shaved, and then headed downtown to the offices of the local newspaper. The kids would forget there was one or think they had nothing to learn from someone tracking bake sales and little league in a backwater, but they were wrong about that. There are canny people everywhere and a good one to start with is the editor of the local weekly.

This one was at his desk, reading through the edition he'd just got out that morning, Saturday. His name was Mike Leachman and I could tell he'd worked through the night from the patchy shave he'd given himself, earlier in the washroom of the *Record's* offices, I figured. He looked up when I came through the door and knew right away who I was. What I was.

There are people you take an instant liking to and Mike Leachman was one of them. His desk was on the other side of a chest-high counter dividing the office in two. Behind him was a larger room with the printing presses and rolls of newsprint; you could see them through a door and hear the clatter of machinery. He was perhaps thirty-five, balding, and with one front tooth chipped. It gave him a Huck Finn type smile. He didn't get up from his desk. He closed his eyes for a second and then pointed to a wooden chair on his side of the counter. That's when I noticed his hands, soft white fingers fluttering at the ends of long thin wrists, never idle.

"There's tea," he said, pointing to a Silex pot on a hot plate. "Can't stand coffee." He lifted a white mug at his elbow and sipped from it.

I found an ashtray. When I told him my name, Mike said he had an uncle the same, only shortened from Manville. He said he'd been up all night with the Linotyper, scrambling the layout at the last minute to fit in the bits he'd added about the shootings. I noted that, *shootings*. He rotated one hand and showed me the ink-stains on his fingers. "Don't usually mess in that end of the business myself," he said.

The knot of his tie was pulled snug even though his shirt was beginning a second day's wear, so right off I think here's a man you can rely on. He passed a newspaper to me, pointing to the piece he'd written Friday night and shoe-horned onto the front page of the *Red Rock Record*. Sensible prose, if somewhat blunt and flat. Rebecca (Becky) Peterson and Thomas (Tommy) Piper had suffered wounds from a shotgun early Friday morning. Becky had died instantly, Tommy was in critical condition at the Red Rock General Hospital. Hank Peterson was being held by the local police. No more than I'd heard from the brief radio reports through the static on the drive up.

"Crazy to say, but those shootings were plain bad timing," Mike said. "Friday morning is when we do our press run around here so we'd already put this week's edition to bed but had to start over again at the last minute because we wanted the story on the front page. Threw us into a total state." He waved one hand in the air to indicate the general confusion about the place. Then he put his mug down and wiped his lower lip. "I had no time at all to work on that," he added, meaning the headline article. "Virtually a first draft."

I made some sympathetic noises, but I was watching his hands dance from the tea mug to his mouth to the papers on the desk. They reminded me of butterflies, settling on things delicately for a second before fluttering off again, and then I realized what it was they reminded me of, my father's hands. The old man was a whiz with things mechanical, and when he was working at a car motor, say, his fingers literally danced from one place to another.

Only that was an awful memory for me, because thoughts of my father always end up spinning back to the day he left us – and my foolish attempts to explain it to myself. I have to close my eyes to wish that day away, and it does not work. I'm left with that horrible image of him staring at me across the car motor, screaming in my face, "You're worse than useless, you're a menace to anyone that comes near you!" I was twelve years old. I had been helping him and had dropped a wrench into the engine, and he was furious. He had reached into the clattering parts of the engine, fished out the wrench, and flung it over my head across the garage, where it struck the wall and fell to the floor with a clang. Neither of us had moved.

I don't recall how long we stood that way, or who moved first, or if the wrench was ever picked up. What I remember is that as we stood there I had the most horrid imaginings. There were gardening tools hanging on the walls in the garage – rakes, hoes, that sort of thing. And an axe. The axe was within reach, and I was in such a white fury that I found myself stepping toward it. I imagined bringing the cold bevelled steel down on his head, splitting the skull the way we'd split frozen stove-wood one winter. I imagined blood and brains spilling out and it thrilled me. He would lie at my feet broken and helpless. I wanted nothing less than to see him dead. Before I knew what was happening the smooth handle of the axe was in my hands.

I didn't do it, of course, but it brought me to a realization very early in life: anyone is capable of doing anything. Murder, rape, bestiality. I had come close to killing my own father with an axe, and if I could do that, anyone could do anything: the guy who fixes your car, the little old lady next door (those fairy tales are right about that), even the preacher with his white collar.

Another trick I've learned about dealing with my memories is to breathe slowly while counting to ten and whispering *all right*. I must have done it that morning because Mike Leachman suddenly asked, "What's all right?"

"The tea," I said, "I don't want any," and adjusted my bottom to the hard-backed chair he'd pointed out on his side of the counter. While he sipped tea and I smoked, he filled me in on things I hadn't got out of the newspaper or radio reports. He told me Becky and Tommy were naked in bed (no surprise), that Hank had been drinking – there was a nearly-empty mickey on the front seat of the car, that Hank had booked off his shift at the mine two hours early, that the weapon was a shotgun, twelve gauge, very messy when fired at close range. There were details about Becky's body, about blood and stuff all over the room too grisly to repeat. No one had been able to talk to Tommy yet – or Hank – but it added up to premeditated murder, no doubt in Mike's mind, and Hank was going to need the sharp lawyer his family in Toronto had hired.

At one point he snorted into his tea. "Sam Johnson is a ruthless bastard. Rumour has it he's had a few locals taken care of over the years. Loud mouths in the union, guys who looked up Becky's skirt when she was in school. He's pig ignorant himself, but he's got what it takes to get his own way."

I nodded and looked about for an ashtray.

Mike added, "It would be easy for a man with his power to arrange an accident, or have someone paid off."

"But it was Hank did the shooting."

"Hank pulled the trigger. Someone set him in motion."

I blew smoke rings in the air. "But it was his daughter got killed."

"A man like Sam is capable of many things. Becky had become what you might call an embarrassment."

We sat in silence for a while. Finally Mike said, "You sure you don't want to go over there? The house, I mean. Before it's locked up?"

We drove over in the Ford, Mike pointing things out on the way: Main Street; the new Woolworth store; the place where they vulcanized rubber for the tires of the Euclid trucks and earth haulers; the granite hill looming in the centre of town, at its peak the electric horn that signalled the end of each shift at the mines as well as noon hour; the Pickerel River; the ball diamonds; the three-storey brick houses on the hillside where the town's upper crust lived; the housing development where Hank and Becky had their place, a wood-frame bungalow much like all the others on the street.

A cop stood on the front steps patting his shirt pocket for a cigarette when we walked up. Mike introduced him as Chief Dixon. I offered him one of mine.

"You're the first of a bad lot, buster," he said, looking me in the eye as he pinched the cigarette between his lips. "Poking into everything."

I muttered something about every man doing the job and struck a match for him.

"Wouldn't have you poking around at all," he said, "if it weren't I got orders." He studied the camera bag I had slung over one shoulder and spat. "I can see it already, reporters stamping through the place, turning things over, and if that's not bad enough, firing questions at me. You'd think I was here to supply every Luke and Lucy with information." He dragged on his cigarette and looked at the glowing end for a moment. He studied me as if waiting for something, and then said, "Anyways, now you're here, you might as well go in. But make it snappy. And for Christ sake don't move anything."

Mike pointed out to me the blood stains in the hallway and the circled spots on the wall above the bed where there were smears of flesh and blood, already hardened to crust. I took a few shots of each and glanced under the bed. There was a rough outline in white chalk where Tommy's body had lain on the floor and another on the bed for Becky. Mike explained that the neighbours who'd found the bodies had cleaned up the floor and shifted Tommy onto the mattress when they discovered he was breathing. You could see where the blood had been smeared about on the floor, enough to make identification impossible. So much for evidence. I kicked the pile of clothes at the foot of the bed. The odour of urine wafted up. I wondered about their last moment, Becky and Tommy's – had they been interrupted in the middle of doing it? I peeked under the mattress. I stood at the window looking at the neighbours' house, wondering if that's the last thing Tommy had seen before he fell to the floor. I went to the other side of the bed and knelt beside Becky's pillow, where I looked back to the doorway and tried to imagine her hearing Hank come down the hall. What was she thinking when he came through the door? I snapped a few more shots. While I knelt there, I smelled something, cordite, and I ran my nose over the pillow to see where it came from. That's when I saw the smudges, one on the edge of the pillow case and the other on the wall just above the headboard of the bed, below the crusted-over flesh and blood. Black grainy stuff like the powder that floats out of the pencil sharpener when you shake it over the garbage can. It didn't catch the eye the way the blood and the bits of flesh on the wall did – they were front page stuff, but it niggled at something in the recesses of my brain, and I should have been smart enough to pursue it. I wasn't. I was already working on my angle, an angle that won me an award, by the way, to my profound and lasting dismay.

When I turned round I saw Mike down the length of the hallway talking with Chief Dixon on the front steps. The cop had the keys to the house in his hand and was flipping them over and over in his fingers. "Okay, buster," he said when I came out, "that's it for you, and good riddance as far as I'm concerned." He locked the door, tried it once, then wheeled on the steps, trying to impress us with his importance. But I could see he knew nothing. They almost never do, small town cops. That doesn't stop them throwing their weight around and making your life miserable. As somebody said, give a man a little rope....

When we got in the car Mike said, "Dixon's okay. He keeps the drunks moving on Saturday nights. Makes sure the union guys don't get totally out of hand. He's firm, and that's what a town like this needs."

I was butting out a cigarette in the ashtray and grunted what could have been mistaken for agreement. In the silence that followed I waited for Mike to say more about Dixon, but he pulled at the knot of his tie and seemed to be lost in thought. We drove in silence past the ball diamonds and over the bridge into the downtown area. I wanted to talk to the neighbours, but not when Mike was present, so I asked him to fill me in on them first and suggested we go to the café for a cup of coffee. That way, I figured, I'd have some background going into the interviews, but could fob Mike off if it looked like I needed to.

We sat in the booth at the far end of the restaurant and drank tea that coated my tongue and made swallowing difficult. "Roy Buechler," Mike said, "is a decent man, but his business is on the skids. So are lots of others, if it comes to that. He's not openly bitter, but he drinks a bit too much." Mike was in full flight. Whatever they put in that tea flushed his cheeks and loosened his tongue. He went on, "For drink your man is Lyle Butler, who starts the day with a bottle of dry sherry mixed with orange juice, a sure sign of the alcoholic. Steady hands, however, and always willing to oblige with a prescription, even after hours. The best pharmacist we've ever seen in this town, which explains why there's no talk about Lyle's little eccentricity."

I was wondering what that was when Mike said, "Hsst, here he comes now." He tipped his chin toward the door where a middle-aged man wearing a black fedora was just entering the restaurant. He placed both hands palms down on the counter. Cashmere jacket, rings on three fingers of each hand, glittering in the overhead lights, I knew what Mike was getting at right away. I wondered what such a man was doing in Red Rock. Skeletons in his closet, for sure. He was too far away for me to catch much of a look at his face and he didn't look into the room while Irene poured out a couple cups of take-away coffee, so I had to wait for that until later. Intriguing.

The noon crowd was beginning to fill the booths of the restaurant and I realized suddenly that I was exhausted. We paid for the coffee and I dropped Mike at the *Record* and went back to the Rockton for a nap. I had a plan of action. In the evening I'd call on Tommy Piper at the hospital, then set up an interview with Roy Buechler to get his version. I had an idea I'd spend Sunday sniffing around town before digging through files at the *Record* Monday. By then I'd be ready for Lyle Butler. From the beginning I knew he was the key to the story I was after.

I dropped off right away, and when I woke it was nearly six and I was ravenous. At the front desk I asked about sit-down meals, and the dyed redhead at the desk told me the pickerel at the Rain River Hotel across from the railroad station got raves from visitors. I decided to walk. I've always felt that's the only way to know a place, really know it, to walk from one end of it to the other.

The first couple hundred yards I walked on the gravel verge, noticing how the ground – gravel, sand, clay, everything – was tinged red with iron dust. It coated the wheels of the cars that passed, too, and when I crossed the tracks into the town proper, I looked closely at the buildings and saw that it formed a skirt of stain on the few feet of stucco nearest the ground. Iron. The soil was permeated with it. In the Québec Shield towns the water tasted of sulphur, but I hadn't noticed that in Red Rock. The sky was high and blue, though the air was cold for an autumn day. But people were out on the streets, lots of kids, I noticed, riding bikes and playing games with balls and sticks. Their sneakers were coated in red dust.

I passed the cemetery, lots of fresh graves with cut flowers, and I could not help wondering if the grave digger had to hack through the granite I'd seen everywhere around Red Rock, or if the soil was soft there, as it was along the banks of the Pickerel River. This was the older part of town and the houses showed it, chipped paint, front steps askew from frost heave. Someone had planted elms along the boulevard, but most had died, covered in red rust. A few streets over the houses were newer but more than a few were empty. Mel's Garage and Red Rock 'Recking were rundown tin-roofed places where men smoking roll-your-owns gathered in the front offices, communicating in grunts. I'd seen this all before in mining towns.

Boom and bust: schools empty, houses deserted, cars abandoned, appliances trashed, lives uprooted.

On Main Street the cars were parked diagonally. A faded *For Sale* sign hung in the window of Shaw's Bakery, and Lee's Foods and the Kresge's store were boarded up. Through the window of Peter's Books and Records I saw the clerk, a teenager with red hair sitting cross-legged on a chair reading a magazine; the proprietor of Fred's Hardware leaned on the counter, cleaning his nails with a pocket knife. People were out shopping, putting bags in cars, but the place felt like it was holding its breath, waiting for an explosion. Men and women passed with faces averted, hurrying some place, frightened. I passed The Steep Rock Café, where a few miners sat over coffee and pie. At the far end of Main stood the Union Hall, and just a little past it the Rain River Hotel.

I had two servings of firm sweet pickerel simmered in fresh butter while I made notes in my black book. According to Mike this was an open-and-shut case: jealous husband shoots wife and her lover. The blood and guts made it interesting. If he were doing the story, he'd be working the desperate working-stiff angle, currying (his word) sympathy for the ordinary guy. He had taken pictures of Hank sitting on the steps of his house: shoulders hunched forward, hands on knees, he looked like a child who'd lost something, a victim. So there was something to the angle he favoured. The CBC crew was leaning that way. The kids from the dailies were going for sex and sensational photos – on Friday morning a neighbour had snapped a picture of Becky's body being carried from the house, pearly skin of one shoulder exposed, a bloody arm dangling from the stretcher, and that photo was a scoop, as were interviews of Tommy's pals at the Rockland Hotel, a rugged and brassy crowd, but sexy, in their way. Turns out Tommy had been driving a car that piled into a rock cut a couple years back, killing one of his chums and maiming several others. The kids were having a field day interviewing and photographing them. Red Rock was coming across as pretty racy.

That was all right by me, but I had my own angle to work.

After the pickerel I ate two pieces of delicious blueberry pie with ice cream. The blueberries, the waitress informed me, had been locally picked out at the floodwaters, an area a few miles from town where artificial lakes had been created when the waters of actual lakes had been dredged away from the rich iron deposits, pumped through a pipeline for several miles and dumped into the natural landscape. The second awe-inspiring feat of engineering I'd encountered in a day. I smoked cigarettes and drank coffee. I made notes until I started to doodle. I was looking forward to interviewing Roy Buechler and Lyle Butler. They had messed up the bedroom, but according to Mike were both reliable and sincere men, liable to tell you things that were more significant than they realized. I wondered if any of the kids had interviewed them yet and decided it didn't matter even if they had. On my walk over I had seen a few of them going into the Rockland Hotel, and if I wasn't mistaken another handful was watching TV in the lobby of the Rain River.

I stuck my nose in on the way out. They were watching a ball game, hooting at fielding plays and arguing about statistics. A few nodded in my direction and someone made room on the big sofa but I declined with a polite wave. They expected it. I was the hot shot in those days and they were mere kids, so we didn't mix much, though we respected each other. I admired their enthusiasm and they acknowledged my ability to get to the heart of story and cover it with a damning flair.

That's the point when you're a hot shot: someone's to blame. Your job is to find out who, and you accomplish that with zeal, caring nothing who gets trampled along the way. You believe in Truth and you're convinced you're the one to uncover it. As you might guess, it's a philosophy for the young; later in life you know better, and you move slower, recognizing that everyone goofs up and everyone has feelings that can be easily squashed.

I wasn't thinking that when I tracked down Roy Buechler on Sunday afternoon. He and his family had gone to church in the morning, and I caught up to him while he was still wearing his white shirt and tie. His greying hair was cropped short, high over the ears. He indicated we would go outside to talk, so we sat in the backyard on wooden lawn furniture and he stretched his legs out, crossing his feet at the ankles. It was a warm fall day, though Roy said it would dip past freezing by nightfall.

He pointed out to me where Hank had planted spruces along the bottom of his yard. Hank, he said, was a dynamo of energy, one of those guys always working on a project. He told me Hank coached his son, Andrew. Roy didn't like sports himself, though he always went to his son's games. From what he could tell, Hank was a good coach. And the kids liked him. As Roy talked, he licked his lips, the sign of the drinker. He looked the neat whiskey type: fire one back, pour the next from the bottle.

I lit a cigarette. "So what can you tell me?" I asked.

Roy studied me a moment. "I can tell you it was ugly in there. There were bits of flesh sliding down the walls and gouts of blood."

"Gouts?"

Roy laughed and shook his head. "I have no idea where that word came from. My years at Saint Joe's, I guess. Parochial school." He laughed again and then added, "Have you seen what happens to the human body when it's hit that close up with shotgun pellets?"

"I can't say I have, no."

"And you don't want to. You don't even want to think about it."

Roy sat up, drawing in his long legs like a praying mantis. His hands were shaking. "There was a big pool of blood on Becky's side of the bed, the size of a serving plate or bigger – from her head – what was left of it." He looked away at Hank's spruces for a moment and then shifted his gaze to me. "You know," he said, "this is making me sick all over. I need a drink – some water."

He had gone pale and when he stood he steadied himself by placing one hand on the stucco wall of the house. He looked as if he needed a glass of the strong stuff.

When he came back a few minutes later he carried a tumbler of water, but I had the impression he'd had a shot while he was in the house. He looked sheepish. I should have told him it made no difference to me. Whatever the case, he seemed determined to tell me what he knew. He started right in again. "Tommy lay face down on the far side of the bed. You've seen the room – over near the window. All he had on was shorts – and he'd filled them. People do that when they've been shot. I was in Italy in '44. I've seen that." Roy nodded knowingly and took a sip of water. "The urine was mixed with blood on the floor – awful colour, worse smell – and it was running under the bed toward the hallway. That's the stuff we cleaned up, Lyle and me. So we wouldn't slip in there – and so no one else would."

"We don't need to discuss the gore and so on," I said. "I was thinking more about the people, the personalities involved."

Roy looked surprised. "Oh," he said, "Becky was a piece of work. Right on the edge, if you know what I mean."

"I'm not sure I do."

"I won't say she deserved what she got. Some

would. I'd say you play around behind a man's back, it catches up to you, sooner or later."

"You didn't like her?"

"That's not really the point." Roy paused. "The point is Hank found out about her little trysts and blim-blam, end of story."

"Hank was that kind of guy – jealous, rash, easily angered?"

"It went on a long time. There were rumours. Ask Dixon. Most guys would have flown off the handle sooner. Hank did what a man in his position does. She was making a fool out of him, wasn't she? He just did what was natural."

"But otherwise he was all right, a regular guy, would you say?"

"He had a temper, I'll grant you that. We argued politics a few times. He worked himself into a state. He was easily provoked."

"I imagine working in those mines makes you that way."

"You mean the crap those men have to put up with – the noise, the dirt, the long hours underground?"

"And the tension between the miners and the bosses. Confrontations."

"They know what they're getting into."

"Do they?"

Roy studied me a moment. "It's a filthy occupation, I'll grant you that. All that red dust. Like blood, you could say. I've spent a decade of my life washing that stuff away. You never really get the stains out."

I had the impression that we were wandering. I

inhaled a few times and said, "Yet this regular guy, this otherwise level-headed ordinary joe one day just up and blows away his wife and her – and her boyfriend?"

"Yes. Jealousy. He just lost it there."

"Like most guys would in the same circumstances – is that what you're saying?"

"I'm saying who knows what they might do given the right provocation? Do you?"

I was making a note in my little black book. I waited for Roy to say more, and when he didn't I asked, "It was Becky's and Tommy's, the blood?"

"Naturally."

"Hank himself was not injured?"

"No, no. He was rattled and all, but no, not hurt." Roy studied me a moment and then said, "You're one of those who think Lyle and me did wrong cleaning up in there, aren't you? I've heard that. But at the time it seemed the only thing to do. The right thing."

"Judging what others do," I said, "is a bad tactic in my business. I leave that to psychiatrists – and philosophers."

Roy snorted. "In the past few days," he said, "our little town of Red Rock has been overrun by philosophers."

I had pegged him for a weak man who wanted you to tell him how he'd failed so he could wallow in that and wheedle out of responsibility, but I saw Roy had more grit than that. Good for you, I thought. I leaned forward and asked, "Did Tommy say anything before the ambulance came – anything at all?"

"Not a word. I don't even think he groaned."

"What about Hank?"

"Stuff about Becky. Odd stuff. He seemed so insistent. *That was not my wife.*" Roy ran one hand back through his hair and shook his head, as if trying to recall exactly what Hank had said but could not do it. Then he said, "It was shock. He was talking about the way she looked."

"He was upset about how she looked?"

"He wasn't angry, if that's what you're getting at. Not when I saw him."

"You would not think....He'd just shot his wife."

We were silent for a few minutes. Roy stared off across the grass, and I wondered if he had liked Becky and decided he did not. Finally he said, "You know, Hank was one of those guys boiling over with suppressed passions, but no one really knew Becky, even though she grew up in this town and all. She didn't seem to have friends. She was a beauty, and they seem to scare other women away." He drew one hand across his mouth. "No wait," he said. "Maybe Madge at the hospital. And Kelly Spelchak, the babysitter, a kid but a smart one. She was over there most days. If any one knew Becky, she did."

"To get back to Hank for a minute. He had the gun in his possession – when you first saw him?"

"He did. I took it from him and gave it to my son." Roy smiled. "Made sure there were no shells in it first."

"And that was all Hank said? Nothing about being glad he'd done it, or ashamed he'd done it? Or whether anyone had said anything in there?"

Roy stroked his chin. "Nothing. But then we weren't asking like you are. We wanted to get him out of there. Do what we could for Becky and Tommy. Let me remind you, there was stuff all over the floor, we were slipping in it; we didn't know if Tommy was going to die on us any second; it was chaos in there. We'd just seen a woman with her head blown off. At first we weren't certain Hank was not injured. There was blood everywhere. We hustled him along, even though he was babbling about Becky and what not. Understand?"

"Well, then, going back earlier, what about when you first arrived, did Hank look odd to you?" This was a leading question, the kind lawyers cannot get away with but journalists can. I was building my profile of the deranged husband, thinking that I could make Hank sympathetic as well as a figure who demonstrated my theory that anyone is capable of any evil.

"He was sweating, and he had a blank look on his face, but then who wouldn't, after something like that?" Roy took a gulp of water, dribbling some down his chin. "There were two shots, whoomp, whoomp. We're used to blasting around here, at the mines, but these were different sounds, cleaner, and less, less what? *Resonating,* is that the word?"

"I see. So you knew right away they were gun shots?"

"Not right away, no. You hear the first one and you think backfire or gas tank explosion. It catches you off guard – so unexpected. Then the second one comes, a sort of delayed echo, and it registers – gun shots, gun fire."

I'd been watching Roy's lips; he hardly opened his mouth to speak. In leaning forward to hear him, I realized there was something I wanted to get at here, but I couldn't put it into a useful question. It wasn't about Hank, though I knew it was important to his story, but I was dogged in my determination to pursue *my* story, so the only thing I could think to ask had to do with the way things had happened, so I asked, "And then what?"

"Then I ran to the house. My wife shouted for me to be careful, but I was halfway out the door."

I thought to myself no, Manny, this isn't what you're after, but I couldn't say what I was after, so I made a note in my little book: *gunshots*. I smoked some more, hoping for inspiration, but none arrived. "Is there anything else," I asked Roy, "that you can think of?" A feeble question.

He seemed to be waiting for this because he cleared his throat and leaned back in his chair before speaking. "Only that people understand that you aren't accustomed to running into houses and finding bleeding bodies. Only that your heart's pounding and your mouth is dry and you're thinking to yourself what the hell's happened here, and when you see the dismembered bodies of people you've known for years you panic a bit and want to vomit but you're trying to be a decent citizen and a good neighbour so you don't, not right away, anyway, you do your best, you try to save somebody's life, you're not thinking of legal technicalities and the niceties of evidence, you're thinking shit here's Becky Peterson with half her head gone and Christ there's Tommy Piper bleeding to death, Hank looks like a zombie, what in God's name can I do. It's like the front – different conditions are in effect."

"Easy," I said.

Roy's face had become beet red and his hands, which he'd raised in the air in front of his face, shook like leaves in an autumn wind. "Ordinary rules are suspended."

"I'm sorry," I said, "if I suggested you'd done wrong."

"I'm no hero," he blurted. "Who is?"

That took me by surprise because officially I am, though I didn't say it and never do, but it's not because I'm ashamed or something. I'm proud of the fact, even of the plaque they gave me, and days when I despair about my miserable existence I have this to think of – there was a day in my life when I saved the lives of five kids. That was the year after the Asbestos strikes, and I was covering a story in Toronto, about heroin infiltrating Kensington Market. I was keen to blame the Chief of Police, if I recall.

I was walking along the street about midday, lost in thought when a woman came running along the sidewalk toward me. I was stunned because her housecoat was flapping as she ran and she was barefoot, no shoes, no socks. "Fire," she screamed at me, "it's on fire." I remember thinking how revolting the woman's hair was, long and tangled, a peroxide job with black roots. She pointed to a house. It was a two-storey frame building with wood siding, and it was ablaze. Smoke billowed from the upstairs windows. By this time she had my wrist in her grip, nails piercing my flesh and was screaming into my face. "Those kids are in there, those boys."

I bounded up the stairs and started yelling "Get out, get out!" The rooms downstairs were empty, the kitchen filled with black smoke. I dropped to one knee, pulled my shirt tail out, and held it over my mouth. On the stairway I found three boys, the oldest ten or so, standing holding the banister, wide-eyed with terror, and I grabbed two by the collar and shoved all three in front of me toward the door. By the time we got there the smoke was overpowering. We stood on the front steps hacking and wiping our eyes. I looked at their bare feet, their brown teeth and dirty faces. Urchins, I recall thinking, right out of Dickens. But I felt good about them.

Then the woman grabbed my shoulder. "Two more," she screamed. I looked from her to the boys. It seemed impossible. But she was shoving me back through the door. Inside the smoke had thickened. I dropped to my knees again, peering around. I tore off my shirt and used it to breathe through, making for the steps that led upstairs. In a closet up there I found the other two, the little ones, huddled together, crying, and I carried them under my arms like footballs to safety.

Afterwards people asked me *What were you thinking when you went back in there?* and the answer is I was not. If I had been thinking I wouldn't have gone back in. Thinking in the ordinary way, the way people mean when they ask that question. After the woman screamed *Two more!* my mind fixed on things, that was it. It fixed on phrases like *Breathe through your shirt, keep your face down, steps one at a time, if you have to jump, pick a window above the garage, bend your knees.* Phrases that echoed in my ears and seemed at the same time to be floating in the air in front of me. It's impossible to explain. Something clicked inside me, so that my brain stopped working and instead riveted on certain fundamentals. I was not thinking but acting.

I call what happened to me then The Tic.

Whatever the case, it made me a hero. The kids were saved, the woman wept for the photographers. I got my picture in the paper with my arms around the boys, broken brown teeth, the works, and for a day or two my story was headlines. The mayor gave me a plaque. I spoke on the CBC about how it feels to be a hero. I mentioned The Tic, but I did not discuss the down side.

It had occurred to me while I was being toasted as hero that the same tic I had experienced took over when Rocket Richard brought his stick down on Hal Laycoe's head, the beginning of the so-called Montréal Riots. The Rocket was not thinking. So when people said later *What were you thinking?* it was the wrong question. He wasn't thinking. The question was out of bounds. Same for Hank. And afterwards when he told people *I wasn't thinking,* trying to make sense of what had happened, their retort in their best irritated mother's tone would be *No you weren't, were you?* as if that settled the matter.

The thing is you cannot will yourself to think like you can will yourself to drink castor oil, or stomach a visit from in-laws. Rage and constipation don't equate. Yet we assume thinking is the most important thing we do, when a little familiarity with animals tells us that it is not. Hank Peterson acted. And despite all the talk in the papers and court rooms about premeditated murder, and of temporary insanity, the fact is Hank was *not thinking* in circumstances where most people would not think. No. He was *acting,* which is exactly the opposite sort of thing.

Ugly but true.

I don't enjoy these thoughts any more than the next man, and when I looked at Roy Buechler that day I knew he would not only find them disturbing but decide I was a sicko to boot. So I took up his offer of a glass of water and when we had sat for five more minutes in the tepid fall air, thanked him for his trouble. He showed me to the door and clasped my hand in his, a wet, warm, soft hand that went with the blood-shot eyes.

When I got back to the Rockton I went over my notes. The story I'd been hoping to write was coming together and I felt good about it: Hank had been a sweet neighbourly guy who had suddenly gone berserk. It was a fresh angle and a good one. I already had the first paragraph of my story written and a snappy lead to open: *The Stranger Within.* All I needed were statements from Tommy Piper and a juicy quotation or two from Lyle Butler.

I got nothing from Tommy Piper, who was only semi-conscious, but a shapely nurse wearing pink lipstick told me all about the wounds in his back and skull, and I figured from that that he'd been shot trying to get out of bed or when he was already standing beside it, turning away from Hank. The nurse said the police had been unable to question Tommy and that the doctors felt he was days away from being ready to do anything except sip soup. We didn't know then that he would never speak again and spend the remainder of his life in a wheelchair. There was only one question I had for him, in any case. As I stood talking with her I noticed the nurse, Madge, the tag on her uniform read, was not wearing a ring, and I felt that old desire to sit across a table at a café chatting mindlessly with a pretty woman over coffee as the hours slipped past. That's what I most missed about women, and I recall intending to ask Madge out for coffee when I came back to question Tommy.

In the morning I tried a greasy spoon I'd noticed in the older part of town when I was walking around on Saturday night. The eggs were awful but the coffee hot and the toast done the way you get it in England, brought to the table unbuttered for you to butter when you please. I had two orders. After, I did some reading in the offices at the *Record,* items on the strikes in Red Rock going back a few years, pieces on the police chief, on the hockey teams Hank played for, on the Johnson family. This was background, mostly, the meat and potatoes stuff you need to fill out a story.

I went back to the house. I hate playing detective, but I do have my own take on the old scene-of-the-crime business, though you may laugh at it. In my view, every crime scene radiates an aura. I like to tap into that aura. I find a comfortable place to sit, cross my legs under, close my eyes, and let my mind seep back to where I start to relive the thing. A kind of dreaming. It sounds goofy, I know. The thing is, it works.

I picked a sheltered spot in the Petersons' back yard, under some of the spruces Hank had planted, a place where I wouldn't be noticed by neighbours. I got out my notebook, opened it to the pages where I'd written my notes, and closed my eyes. This is the trick, I've discovered. Total relaxation. I emptied my mind, trying not to think at all, but submitting myself to the sounds of birds and insects and the sensation of the warm autumn sun on my legs.

The shotgun was a twelve gauge with two barrels, and Roy and everyone else had heard two shots, that much was clear. My mind wandered around that fact, picturing Hank (a man's form, I hadn't met him then) moving down the hallway toward the bedroom. I took Becky's perspective. She would have heard floorboards creaking; I had when I walked down the hallway. Perhaps Tommy did, too. They would have seen Hank at the threshold, shotgun in hand. Would he have raised it to his shoulder to fire? Tommy was hit high, buckshot catching his back and neck but not his buttocks. That suggested the gun was fired from Hank's mid-section, barrel tilted upward. And it made sense. You don't need to aim at a target as big as the human body from twenty feet away. I took that in: Tommy rising from the bed, seeing him half turn as Hank pulled the trigger, his body rotating with the impact of that first blast. I saw Hank standing with the smoking gun propped against one hip. His face would be set grimly, a rictus, but Becky's would be scaling the emotions. Perhaps she cried out. Somewhere in there Hank must have turned the gun on her. I pictured her face, recalling it from photos, sharp clean features framed by black hair, eyes widening with horror after the first blast, her mouth forming an O. She might have tried to sit up, scrabbling on one elbow to an upright position. She would have been seeing a totally different Hank than she'd ever seen before – a man possessed by black emotions. What would she have thought, looking down the barrel of the shotgun? Would she have tried to reason with Hank? Called out the name of her son – her lover? Begged for mercy?

There were a lot of questions to be answered. I breathed deeply for a while and felt my heart lugdubbing in my chest. Sitting in silence this way I heard the smoker's rattle in my lungs and ran my tongue over my teeth, sensing the buildup of nicotine. I wished I could quit. Then I had a small insight. All along I'd been thinking that Becky was terrified of Hank, cowering, but what if she'd got past the point where she gave a damn, what if she were in a fury at him as soon as he came into the room, and cursing after he'd shot Tommy? I'd been wrestling with how a man like Hank came to turn a gun on the woman he loved, but I realized then that her anger could have pushed him over the edge, if he was teetering on it. I ran that over my mind for plausibility, and decided it was all part of Hank's transformation that morning into the murderer within us all. I wondered what in his background might point in that direction, and it suddenly occurred to me that a man who plays hockey might have a serious mean streak. I'd have to check on that.

I opened my eyes and stretched my legs out in the grass. Dew was beginning to form. Roy was right, it turned cool toward the evenings. I walked round the house, glancing in the windows, and sat on the cement front steps, steps, Roy had informed me, Hank had constructed himself, building the forms out of rough lumber, then wheel-barrowing the concrete from the backyard where he'd mixed it by hand.

Roy had said the shots sounded like blasting from the mines, whoomp whoomp, but that he hadn't thought of them as shots at first. That puzzled me. I wondered if this Lyle Butler had heard them and what more he could tell me. It was clear that he could confirm Roy's notion that Hank was deranged that morning, a notion that fit in well with my pet theory those days. Whatever the case, I decided to interview him as soon as possible, that night if I could, so I went back to the Rain River for more pickerel and plotted my strategy.

All along I'd been thinking that I would have to come on strong with Lyle Butler. Like everyone else in Red Rock he was suspicious of all of us big city types who had descended on the town, and protective of neighbours and friends. No doubt ready to lie for them. They protected him. It made sense. So I'd been biding my time, letting him work himself up about the possibility of being publicly exposed. Make him think his own ass was on the line. I'd been thinking that once he was in a fine sweat about that he'd tell me things he might otherwise be inclined to hide. To get me off his back, if nothing else. So my first instinct was to go after Lyle Butler, guns blazing.

I don't know what made me change my strategy, it could be the fact I'd spooked Roy Buechler and learned little from him, or perhaps an intuition that a queer was liable to be more helpful to me as friend than enemy. Perhaps I'd just seen a weariness in the man as he stood at the lunch counter at The Steep Rock Café and couldn't go after him the way I'd been planning. Whatever the case, I decided to pretend I knew nothing, even come on thick, if necessary.

It was past nine before I paid my bill (it was raspberry pie that night, scrumptious with whipped cream), and started walking toward the apartment where Lyle Butler lived, directly across the street from the Petersons'. I'd waited that long to let him relax into the evening a bit, kick off the slippers, take an extra drink. I figured if he was mellow and not forcing himself to concentrate, he'd be less inclined to jumble up the facts or resist my questions, and I might learn something.

I stood outside his apartment door listening, and when I'd decided he was alone, knocked gingerly, to relinquish the initiative. In most interviews one party or the other takes control, usually the interviewer – though Sam Johnson types never let that happen – and I wanted to make sure that between us Lyle Butler had every chance to take the upper hand. He came to the door almost immediately but seemed surprised to find a stranger there. I was wearing a top coat against the chilliness of the evening.

Without his fedora on he didn't look as old as when I'd seen him earlier at The Steep Rock Café, though his reddish hair was thinning. He was angry, as I'd expected. Before I could introduce myself he said *reporter* in a way that curled his lower lip.

I hadn't expected the anger to crystallize so fast. I said in a level voice, "I want to explain to our readers how anyone can do something horrible on the spur of the moment but still be as sane as you or me." I was searching my coat pockets for a cigarette. By that time we had crossed into the living room. It was furnished in deco style: glass and chrome. I glanced around, spotting immediately the brandy snifter near the chair where he'd been sitting, watching TV, it appeared. I tried not to notice. I asked him about Hank's state of mind.

"State of mind," he mused. He seemed confused. He thought about it for a moment and then said, "He seemed to go through –"

" – through transformations?"

"Yes. First one thing, then another."

"But he was dressed as usual?"

"Boots, a work shirt. He must have come straight home from the pits."

I was concentrating, noting each word, every inflection. These were the details I was after, the things that would help build up my portrait of Hank. I asked, "Did he say anything?"

"Something about Becky." He waved one hand in the air. "Confused things. The best I could make of it was he was shocked by the way her face looked." He looked at me oddly, as if he were about to clam up, but he went on, "I don't know quite how to put it. He was –"

I leaned forward.

"*Disconnected,*" he blurted out. And then he added, "You know how ordinary lives unravel, you witness it all the time, but that's what makes us different. Hank was the first person I saw go through that transformation. He was going along nicely, thinking he had things under control, when really they weren't, everything was all just waiting to come apart on him. So when he found out Becky was slutting around, he just didn't think of consequences, he didn't consider what would become of young Scott and so on." He looked around suddenly and blushed, realizing he'd gone into a tirade. Then he said, "I'm not making very much sense, am I? I don't know…."

I knew. He needed that snifter of brandy. "Just one more question," I said. I could hardly believe he'd made that speech, a speech I could turn into the centrepiece of my story. I was pushing my luck but I asked, "Where did you first see Hank that morning?"

"Inside the house. In the hall outside the bedroom."

"Not *in* the bedroom?"

"No. Minutes had elapsed. By the time I got there, Roy was leading him down the hall."

I knew I'd gone too far. "Right," I said. "Right." What I was thinking was *wrong, Manny, wrong wrong.* We were straying into other territory now, not filling in the profile of Hank the way I had hoped. He was only telling me details about the chain of events, about the sequence. My brain was foggy with tiredness, so for a moment I forgot myself, and when he came into focus again I realized that Lyle Butler had raised one hand as if to fend me off. I must have taken a sudden step toward him as I asked, "You weren't afraid of him – of what he might do?" For a second I didn't know why I'd asked it, but the something that had been niggling at my brain when I'd seen the smudges was back again, though I was too stupid to see it at the time. Too much in love with my own ideas.

"No," Lyle Butler said. "He had the gun but we were not afraid."

"Yes," I said, meaning, no, that's not what I want to hear. In desperation I asked, "What I mean is, what about the shots?"

"There were two. Like *kaboom, kaboom*. You know." He mouthed the sounds.

"Yes," I said. I had no idea why I'd asked that but I was wishing I had a cigarette to give me something to do with my hands. Something led me to ask, "How far apart were they – the shots?"

He seemed to be taken by surprise because he stepped back again, but he said, "There might have been a gap between them." He paused. "Yes, I think there was a gap."

I was digging around in my coat pocket for cigarettes and missed it, see, the statement that should have made me cry *aha* and ferret out the truth in that story instead of relying on my stupid predisposition to think I already knew it. The Truth, according to Manson Welch, special correspondent. But I was gloating by that time, imagining my article on "The Stranger Within," an article that would galvanize *Weekend* readers' imaginations and win me a reporter's prize. I asked, trying not to sound as triumphant as I felt, "Would you mind if I lit up a cigarette?"

Outside it was not as cold as had threatened and I stood on the sidewalk in front of the apartment block, smoking and studying the sky. The moon was bright silver, as were the stars, a whole chorus of them you don't usually see in the city. I was starting to appreciate why people stayed on in Red Rock even when they had the chance to move. As I said, it was elemental up there: rocks, trees, lakes, stars. The sky seemed closer. Looking up, I saw a shooting star light up suddenly, and I tracked its parabola overhead until it blazed out over the mines to the east. The dull glow of lights came from that direction and I recalled the mines operated around the clock.

I'd asked Roy about the floodwaters and he had given me directions to a lookout location near the open pits, so I decided to drive out there to clear my head. I was too excited for bed.

To get to the lookout site at the open pits you had to drive through the floodwaters. These were manmade lakes about ten miles from the sites of the open pits. When a rich body of iron ore was discovered on the floor of a lake the mining companies hired dredges to pump the water out of the lake so the miners could get at the ore. The water, along with whatever fish, plant, and animal life survived, was carried in a pipeline that was three feet in diameter to the location and dumped on top of whatever was there, muskeg, stunted trees, beaver lodges, and so on. This area became a new lake, a lake with the stumps of trees sticking out of it like the photos you sometimes see of No Man's Land, a place where the locals fished and sometimes swam.

From the lookout site the mining company had built you saw the entire operation: far off the dredges pumping out a lake, in the middle distance the conveyor belts, and immediately below you, the bulldozers loading trucks with iron ore. There were overhead lights, a network illuminating the vehicles. The drop from where I stood down to the floor of the pit had to be several hundred feet, truly staggering. I'd expected something impressive but not on that scale, and the trucks down there, thirty-five tons, I learned later, seemed like Dinky Toys in five-and-dime stores. The pit I was looking into had once been a lake, you could see on the walls of the rock face opposite the high water marks from centuries of geological change, and below them the striations of differing rock deposits. Everything was tinged red from iron. The bed where the trucks and bulldozers circled each other, stirring up the ore, was a rust table. Their tires were coated in it. I perched on the restraining fence and smoked, fascinated by the work going on below. After the lake had been drained, layer after layer of iron ore had been peeled off by bulldozers.

I missed the metaphor of getting to the bottom of things, as hot shots will.

I thought I alone understood then what no one else did: how Hank the good guy could kill his wife and leave his child motherless. Most people were having a difficult time squaring his all-American behaviour with the double murder. No doubt they'd heard the grisly details about blood and body parts and seen the photos in the papers and read the kids' purple prose. It was difficult to square the images created by those descriptions with the Hank they saw hauling dirt in his backyard and carting the baby about on his shoulders. That was the simple logic of their hearts, and I was too absorbed by my own thinking to see they were right. Even during the trial, when the town doctor who acted as coroner tried to float the theory that Hank had not shot Becky, I had smiled in my patronizing way from the back of the courtroom and thought *local yokel.* None of the kids took him up, either – they were still wringing the sensational sex angle for all it was worth. But there were the smudges, there were those otherwise illogical things Hank muttered when he first came out of the bedroom, and most important, there was the time lapse between the first and second shots. Hank had not shot Becky. She had done it herself. If I'd put it all together then, as I have since, I would not have won the journalism prize and Hank would not have come to trial for a death he had no part in. But that is not what happened.

Over the next few weeks I filed the articles that made "The Stranger Within" a catch phrase around news rooms in the following decades. We discovered Tommy Piper had nerve damage in his spinal column and had lost the use of his legs. We saw Becky buried. Kelly Spelchak, a girl who had babysat for Hank and Becky, was taking care of Scott, though the Johnsons seemed to be in legal custody of the child, Hank's parents being off in Europe until Christmas. We discovered Tommy Piper's vocal chords were permanently damaged: he might never talk again. Hank was acquitted on the grounds of *crime passionnel,* a form of temporary insanity, a verdict that fit well with my own theories. We filed our final pieces and left Red Rock for good. In the spring I was awarded the top prize given to journalists for my five-part profile of Hank Peterson, loving father, doting husband, committed little league coach – and killer. I was the hot shot of the hot shots. Nate at the *Weekend* gave me two raises to keep me from jumping to Southam, and CBC offered me a ten-minute weekly spot on national radio, a job I declined right off.

Everything was going swimmingly for me when two years later the Red Rock episode came crashing down on me. Literally. I was covering a story in northern Québec, where a lumber mill had caught fire and then spread into the forests of the Shield. I was at the peak then, living on accountable advances and wheeling about in rented cars provided by the *Weekend.* I'd driven up from the city and forced my way into the mill's offices, snapping photos and firing questions at the executives before heading down the highway to see the blaze in person. It was a conflagration, as it turned out, but that wasn't what interested me. My interest lay in getting to the bottom of things, in pinning the blame on someone. I was cocky. I was very sure of myself, as only the young can be. A match had been dropped, I figured; or a machine left unattended; someone forgot to do a regular maintenance check of electrical wiring. The cause may not be clear to the hot shot but this much is: there is a cause and someone is to blame. That's what you're digging for: the person to blame. You hope it's a company executive, someone you can embarrass, bring down a peg or two, but you'll settle for the shift boss, or the stiffs working the machines, or even the lowly office clerk – whoever – as long as you get your story.

After I'd got my photos of the fire I drove back to the town to interview the men who worked in the lumber mill: I had a hunch one of their bosses was to blame for the fire. I was driving down a gravel road when I heard a thump under the car, like a large metal part had broken off, then some awful grinding noises. I was five miles from town and that far from the fire. Naturally, it pissed me off to be short-circuited when I was just getting going on my story. I pulled over. Smoke was coming from the rear end, but I couldn't see under the car well enough to tell if the damage was serious. Being a hot shot I was in too big a hurry to wait for help or think the situation through. I chucked off my jacket and rolled up the sleeves of my shirt. I got out the jack. When I had the car up, I removed one wheel and crawled underneath. I felt around near the axle, thinking a seal had blown – there was a lot of oil around – but just as I was getting a fix on the problem, I heard crunching sounds. I thought to myself *Is the jack slipping?* I placed both hands flat on the ground and shoved, pushing myself across the gravel to get clear of the car. I was right. The car came straight down with a dull thud. The rear axle sank into the gravel in exactly the spot my chest had been a few seconds earlier. Pieces of loose metal dropped off the undercarriage of the car and puffs of white dust floated up from the road like smoke. In the dust from the undercarriage there were clear prints of my palms and fingers where I had placed my hands so as to scramble free. I was partly pinned by the underside of the running board, and I was in a state of near hysteria, but after a minute or two of wriggling and tearing the skin off my one shoulder, I worked myself free.

I lay on my back staring up at the sky. It was blue, I remember. I lay there for some time with the gravel digging into my back, thinking.

They call that a near-death experience. It changed my life. I don't know why. It had nothing to do with the story I was writing or with some philosophy of life I thought through then or since. It wasn't even anything I articulated to myself. But I stopped being a hot shot that day. As I lay there under the car it had suddenly come to me: Hank Peterson had shot Tommy Piper in a fit of fury, but the smudges over the bed were at the wrong angle for Hank to have pulled the trigger on Becky. Something else had happened in that bedroom, and if I had been less wrapped up in my hot-shot theories I might have found out what occurred between the first and second blasts from the shotgun, quite possibly that Becky had wrestled with Hank for the gun and accidentally blown off her own head. Yes, that was it. Becky Peterson killed herself. The hand prints on the window curtain proved the shotgun was not in Hank's possession the whole time he was in the room. Someone else had had it, if only for a moment.

I was shaking. I wasn't sure whether it was from

what had happened under the car, or for being such an idiot in Red Rock. I wondered how many other people knew how big a sham the whole stranger within thing really was.

When I'd finished shaking I sat by the side of the road, hugging my knees with my arms. I smoked some cigarettes, trying not to think, just feeling the sun on my face, listening to the insects buzz round my head. I walked the five miles back to town, refusing a number of rides. Near the outskirts I sat on a rock outcropping and smoked two or three more cigarettes. Wild roses grew by the side of the road, beautiful pink wild roses. I looked at them and thought *I have no intention of picking you, none.* That felt good.

I filed the story I'd been working on, my one concession to the code of the hot shots, and then I spent a night in the bar, drinking Black Label with mill workers, lumber jacks, and fire fighters. I woke with a hangover and felt good about it. I retrieved my car, got it fixed, drove back to Montréal, and went to talk to my editor about switching from feature news to the book review page. In a month I was doing just that, reading the prose of novelists and writing what I hoped were witty reviews, and suspicious of the man I'd once been.

As I say, it's a story that reflects badly on me. Some mornings when I step from the shower and light catches me just the right way I see in the mirror the scar that runs along my collar bone to the tip of my shoulder where the undercarriage of the car caught me that day up in northern Québec, what the cops call *distinguishing features.*

Jigsaw

Kelly Spelchak:

You will say I should go back and read what that reporter said, about Hank being his own worst enemy, blah blah blah. You will say I was just a kid of sixteen, a miner's daughter to boot, and that I have no idea what I saw back there in Red Rock. Susie Creamcheese meets Jack the Ripper. Maybe so. But I looked into Becky's heart and I saw the darkness.

Point Number One: Scarlet the Harlot.

When I babysat at their place I used to see her washing her hair at the bathroom sink. "A girl's got to keep up her appearance, Kelly," she said to me. She laughed and rolled her eyes. (We were sharing a secret but neither was saying what it was.) She walked around the house humming snatches of Frank Sinatra songs as she dried her hair, rubbing it vigorously on a big white towel, sometimes with a cigarette dangling from her lips. She painted her nails scarlet and when she was getting ready for work she stood at the kitchen counter filing them with an emery board.

"You like this colour?" she asked me one time, "scarlet?"

"Yes."

"Me too. Scarlet the harlot."

She laughed but I did not. I was studying how she lined her eyebrows with black pencil and used some smudgy dark powder beneath her eye sockets to make them seem sunken, a look that was supposed to suggest mystery. She was one part wife, one part mother, and seven-tenths teenybopper.

"Sounds like *no,* the way you say *yes.*"

"I don't know, is what I mean. I don't wear makeup."

"Your old lady won't let you?" Her tone hinted we become conspirators against Mother. Rebels with a powder-puff cause.

"She'd like me to, I think. The fact is, I don't much care for it."

"You don't?"

"Not really. Nor women who wear too much."

"Oho," Becky said. "You're a strange one, Kelly." She laughed, tossing her head back. "Mucho strange, kiddo. Nuts."

People were always saying I was nuts, men with a

shake of their heads, women pursing their lips. It worried me at first because I didn't want the girls at school to think I had weird opinions, like a Mormon or something, so I watched what I said until I realized it was merely that I *had* opinions. I talked to Janet about it and here's what we decided: girls weren't supposed to think, so when adults came across them doing it, they put it down to the influence of rock and roll, or James Dean. So most of the time we pretended not to. *Ditzy,* we called it then. It kept the peace.

One of Daddy's sayings: "Don't stir the pot."

Point Number Two: Becky the Air Head.

"Kelly," Becky said to me once, "that's such a cute name. Did your mother get that out of a magazine?"

"Come again?"

She said, "A movie magazine." Her living-room was awash with them, a library of lust, as well as ashtrays overflowing with cigarette butts and combs spiky with hair. She insisted, "Your mother saw a movie, right?"

"Mother rarely goes to the movies."

"Come on," she said, "that cowboy one – Gary Cooper, one good man."

"I got you now. Grace Kelly."

"Bingo, kiddo." Becky gave me one of her self-satisfied smirks.

"You're wrong," I said, "about that. It was not a movie. Though I am stuck living out Mother's fantasy. Some glamorous fly-boy she met once."

"At least that's romantic. Try the Bible. Try *Re-bec-ca.*"

She virtually spat the name out. I said, "Typical, don't you think, that I'm living out Mother's fantasy?"

"It's typical that you're being hard on your mother."

"You didn't fight with yours?"

"At your age? Too much. About the wrong things. Now I regret it."

We were standing outside Scott's bedroom. Becky had washed her hair and put on a dress, red, with a black plastic sash. I grant her this: she was attractive in a glamorous way. (Hank once called her *divine.*) She flicked on the hall light and was studying herself in the wall mirror, striking poses like Scarlet O'Hara. She and Hank were going out to supper and then dancing, she said, but we could both see him in the yard hauling manure for the trees he'd been planting.

Becky had said things like that before: *regret.* "Come again," I said.

"About regret?" she asked. "Look, it's natural for a girl not to get along with her mother – about clothes and makeup and stuff. Boys. Especially boys. You *should* fight about that."

I nodded. (If you didn't, who would you end up being? Answer: your mother. Pedal pushers, rollers in the hair, Bobbie pins. Not this chickadee, thank you all the same.) "You mean a girl should hate her mother?"

"Not hate," she said, "hate is too strong. Not even dislike."

"Just fight with so you don't become a doormat?"

"You have an odd way of putting things." Becky lit a cigarette and blew smoke stagily into the air above our heads. "You should fight about the little stuff, but you shouldn't fight about the big things." She picked at her lower lip, pinched off a strand of tobacco, and flicked it to the floor. "What am I trying to say?" she continued. "I don't know what I'm trying to say."

We both laughed. "Yes, I do," she said in a minute. "I'm saying there shouldn't be any sneaking around between a girl and her mother. That's it."

"What they don't know won't hurt them?" I said. "Secrets? Deception?"

The words hung in the air for a moment between us while Becky took a drag on her cigarette and eyed me pointedly. "That's right," she said finally. She took another drag. "Let me tell you something here, okay? Show me a girl who has an honest – top to bottom honest, all cards on the table honest – thing with her mother, and I'll show you a girl who won't end up with a jerk."

My first inclination was to ask her if she thought she had married a jerk, but I held back and took in what she was saying. I thought Hank was an okay guy. He smiled a lot, he played with Scott, he didn't swear at me like some of the fathers I babysat for. He had good teeth and dancing eyes. All right, he was a hunk. But I wondered what Becky really thought of him, whether she believed she'd married someone she didn't really like once she got to know him inside out. I wondered, too, how she'd react if I asked her about secrets after marriage. About Tommy the Pied Piper.

"No secrets," I said.

"Not a one."

"That's a tall order," I said, "a tall one and a fat one, too."

"Am I right?" Becky smiled triumphantly. "You know I'm right, kiddo."

Point Number Three: The Third Degree.

I had secrets from everybody, including Mother.

This is painful to admit, and don't think time makes it easier.

About boys, naturally, what else? The eternal secret.

We were allowed to go to movies at the Red Rock Theatre, Janet and I, and school dances, and parties at girl's houses. But that was the extent of it. The tranquilized fifties. And there was always a grilling on the morning after, the Third Degree, Janet called it: which boys were there, who did what with whom, was there drinking? Mother never actually used the word *sex* but it hovered in the air between us like those balloons over the heads of cartoon characters, threatening to explode. It was life before the Pill, and for us girls the terror about *something happening* was palpable. So I didn't tell Mother about Shrevey

Russell that time at Janet's party when we were alone for fifteen minutes in the basement. I had let him put his hands under my sweater, oh sin, and touch me. It was not an unpleasant feeling. But when he asked, "Want to go upstairs," meaning the bedroom, I said no and he was nice enough to let it go at that. *Copping a feel,* the guys called it, even that got you a reputation sometimes. So when Mother grilled me the next day I had lied to her, and it was not a good feeling I carried around in my gut the rest of that day.

But that was not the big secret, no. The big one was Dennis Mandaman, who unlike Shrevey Russell did not come from a house on Spruce Road and did not attend Red Rock High. He had dropped out after Grade Nine. He was an Indian who lived down by the curling rink in a tar paper shack with his six brothers and sisters and a mother who sometimes worked for Andy Buechler's father, ironing shirts. Dennis was good-looking, with those high cheek bones and round brown eyes. And he was a nice guy, plain and simple, quiet-spoken, full of gentle jokes. His hands were soft, though big, the skin that silky olive, like the skin of women from Greece and India and other exotic places in the far east. I loved holding his hand between mine, stroking the fingers. Sometimes we kissed, but that is all we ever managed, a couple of hurried kisses behind the curling rink. (He was as inexperienced as me, I see now.)

I knew it was incredibly, lightning-will-strike-you-down sinful, though, going with an Indian. Mother would have had a fit. She would have had to tell Daddy and who knows what he would have done?

That's what worried me.

Girls, nice girls like Janet and me, were not supposed to go with Indians.

Becky told me about what had happened to her. She went with Johnny Armstead. "It was nothing," she said, "nada, kiddo, we sat in the café a couple of times, we walked down to the ball diamond to see the Sapawe Chiefs playing, his brother was the pitcher." That was enough, though. They had been spotted in public. When Becky came home one night her father took off his belt and slashed her across the legs with it. *No daughter of mine,* kind of thing. She showed me the place where the belt buckle had cut the skin on one calf, an indentation as big as a belly button. Sadistic Sam.

That scared me.

It scared me worse that when Becky and her father got shouting about where she was going a couple of nights later that Sam Johnson had slapped her in the face. That was a regular occurrence for girls in those days, wives too, *thanks I needed that* kind of thing, though not around our house, nothing more than raised voices and shouting. That didn't mean that Daddy did not have a temper. I trembled thinking what would happen if he found out about Dennis Mandaman. So secrets from Mother, and lies, too, little whites and big blacks.

"You gotta keep your nose clean," Becky said. "Or if you can't do that, kiddo, you gotta hold your cards close to your chest."

She was talking about reputation, the big word in those days.

One day Mother and I were busy in the kitchen, listening to the radio and swapping bits of information, *girl talk,* Mother called it.

"She's got a reputation now, but Becky had so much going for her," Mother said. I had the feeling she was working her way around to me. Who was I going with, kind of thing.

"She's done okay for a small town girl," I said.

"Marrying Hank," Mother said, "such a cock-of-the-walk."

"She lucked out there, actually," I said. "Double boxcars."

"A school teacher," Mother said. "No, I correct myself, a failed school teacher, a miner. And Becky with so much promise."

"Oh yeah, tell me about it."

"Oh," she went on, "that modelling thing in Toronto. Remember?"

"As if you would let me forget. But where would that have led?"

"Oh, to big things."

"To the cosmetics counter at Eaton's. Is that what a girl is supposed to be aiming for? Flogging Revlon at overweight, pasty-faced miners' wives?"

"You're getting pretty hoity-toity," Mother said. "You just never know. For one, she might have landed herself a better catch."

"We're talking about fishing, are we?" I snorted. "Or is that your way of saying it's a girl's dream-come-true to bed down with some grunting miner?"

"That smart mouth of yours," Mother huffed, "is going to get you in trouble one of these days, young lady."

"Anyway, she was fed up with local boys," I said. "You may not have noticed, Mother, but these are not stunning specimens of manhood around here. The Red Rock rabble."

"Specimens," Mother sniffed, *"rabble.* Is that what they're teaching you in school, young lady?"

"They're teaching me to think for myself. To wise up to reality."

"Humph," Mother said. She pounded the dough with her tiny fists. She sipped from the cup of cold coffee she kept near her elbow. "And where is that attitude going to get you?"

"Out of Red Rock, one-way ticket, kiddo."

"And into what other mess of trouble, might I ask?"

"Into college, the University of Toronto maybe."

We were rolling out dough for pies and she put her rolling pin down abruptly, wiping her brow with the back of one flour-dusty hand. "Hoh," she said, "that's a good one, college. In Toronto, yet. You are a dreamer."

(That was another secret, my ambitions to attend Victoria College on a scholarship I was hoping to win by scoring among the top hundred in the entrance examinations.) I kept my eyes focused on the dough in front of me, rolling firmly to the edge, the way she had taught me. I kept my mouth shut. That was two years down the road, plenty of time to soften up Mother and get Daddy on my side, even though he was not an easy sell. The problem was he was too straightforward. You threw a hint at him about a birthday present, it better be as obvious as a Nazi at the Jewish Congress or he'd miss it. Men are not big on nuance and subtlety.

Point Number Four: Hank the Lunkhead.

I'd discovered how dumb men could be the summer before.

Things had been coming apart at Hank and Becky's long before either of them knew it. (Another of Daddy's sayings: People can't see past the nose on their faces.) At least Becky did figure out something was wrong after a while. I was babysitting there a lot that summer. There'd been a shortage of nurses at the hospital and Becky could have worked every day, if she'd wanted. As it was she had me come in most afternoons and sometimes on weekends. One day she got home about three. Hank must have been working afternoons. She carried a parcel from Eaton's under one arm and a plain brown bag in her hand.

"Look," she said, opening the package on the living-room sofa. It was a dress, black, strapless. "How about that number?"

"Oh-la-la," I said, "cleavage city."

"You're a real fruitcake, kiddo," she said. "I can never tell whether you mean the things you say, or you're pulling my leg."

"I mean it," I sang back, "each ever-lovin' word."

"That's exactly what I'm getting at," she said, "that tone." She folded the dress back into its box. "Anyways," she went on, "this is for Hank – and for me." She winked in a sexy way and nodded in the direction of the bedroom.

She was Lucy Loose Lips when it came to her personal life. The first time I babysat there she came out of the bathroom and said loudly, "Shit, I forgot to buy condoms." On that occasion Hank was out at the car, getting something from the trunk and I was glad he was, because I don't know what I would have done had he been in the same room as me when she said *condoms*. Passed out, most likely. As it was I turned red from ear hole to bunghole. I pretended I had not heard and busied myself folding a basket of diapers.

Becky continued about what she'd bought. "Only the dress would never do the trick on its own. You understand that, don't you, kiddo?" She looked at me with those bright green eyes and added, "That's why I bought this." She pulled a bottle out of the brown bag. "Rum," she said. "Hank's favourite."

She plunked the bottle on the dining table and flounced out, sticking her nose into the room where Scott was napping, and returning a few minutes later, smoking a cigarette. She said, "I'm trying to tell you something, okay?" She sat on the arm of the sofa and inhaled deeply. The light shone in through the window onto her face, scarved in cigarette smoke, like Rita Hayworth in the movies. "Girl to girl, like, so listen. With men it's never enough to do things to yourself that should please them. You follow?"

I nodded. "That dress, for example."

"Bingo." She took a long drag. "Now if Hank came home with a sharp haircut and smelling of rose water, I'd be pleased." She paused and exhaled. "Pleased, hell, I'd be in seventh heaven." She sighed. "You see what I mean?"

"You'd be all over him," I said, "like a cheap suit."

Becky snorted. "Kiddo," she said, standing, "you're going to make some guy a very unhappy husband." She smirked, and then reached over and gave me a little hug. "I don't mean that," she said, "not really. But I do mean this – with men, you have to be thinking about what they like and constantly doing stuff for them. If you want things between you to go smoothly, you have to figure out what makes your man happy and do stuff for him. For *him.*"

"I get it. Being a wife is being a slave. Cook the meals, wash the kids, meet the hubby at the door in a teddy. Oo-ha!"

"Well," Becky said, "that's just it. Being a woman is –"

"Damn shitty!" I stamped one foot on the floor. "If you ask me."

Becky laughed aloud. "Like you have a choice."

"You could. You might."

"It's what you have to do," she said. "Just watch your mother."

In the weeks that followed Becky mounted a covert campaign to win Hank over. She greeted him at the door when he arrived home from work, all smiles and hugs and kisses. She cooked his favourite foods: mushroom omelets, potato pancakes with sour cream. One day she bought Hank a new tie, green and yellow with mallards on it, very sharp. She showed it to me. (I was just going out the door as Hank came home.) Becky greeted him with the usual big hug and then slipped the tie around his neck. "Hey," he said, "that's really nice." Becky kissed him on the lips and ran her fingers up his neck into his hair.

"You like it?" she asked, rolling those bedroom eyes.

"You bet," he said.

"Really?"

"You bet," he repeated, lifting his arms gently but firmly and slipping out of her grasp. "But go easy, babe, I've got spruces to plant before supper."

He picked the tie off his neck and threw it casually over the back of the sofa, then disappeared into the bathroom where you could hear him whistling over the noise of running water. Becky looked at the tie. She stepped into the hallway and came back with a pair of scissors and snipped it into tiny strips.

Point Number Five: Becky the Bitch.

That's when Becky turned sour. Not that day, or the next, no, but soon after. She stopped greeting Hank at the door. He didn't notice. She began to make a habit of pouring a large rum and Coke before she'd changed out of her nurse's uniform when she got home from work. (I'd be getting Scott up from his nap and I'd hear the refrigerator door open and close and then the familiar tink-tink of ice cubes on glass, a sound that made my teeth rattle like ice cubes themselves.) She'd put a record on and waltz from room to room, humming to herself, oblivious to Scott and me while she had a second drink. Hank did not notice how many bottles of rum were disappearing. And he never looked in Becky's medicine cabinet, so he had no idea about the tranquillizers, either.

I only found out about them because Becky telephoned one Saturday afternoon and asked could I come over and look after Scott. "Hurry," she insisted, "hurry!" And then it sounded like the telephone fell to the floor.

When I got there they were lying on the bed together, the baby flipping through his books and Becky with a damp towel over her face. "I'm not feeling good," she moaned. "Not good at all." She lifted the towel. Her face was greenish, eyes sunk in, and even in the dim light of the bedroom it was obvious she was shaking.

"Should I call the doctor? Tombstone Tom?"

"No," she said, sharply, half sitting. She puffed air into her cheeks, blew it out slowly, and lay back down with a thump. "No," she repeated, with a sigh, "let's keep McCabe out of it." After a while she said through the towel, "Don't worry, I threw up already. I'm okay."

I sat on the other side of the bed and talked to Scott. Becky breathed deeply for a while, then dropped into a light sleep, legs and arms twitching, her mouth making popping sounds. My eyes adjusted to the light. I saw she had been crying. Crumpled tissues were wadded in one of her fists. The make-up around her eyes was streaked and ran down her cheeks. On the night table sat an empty bottle from the pharmacy, Librium. I knew they were tranquillizers.

Scott looked up from his book. “Mommy sad,” he said. He reached his fat arms out to me.

“Yes,” I said, “mommy mucho doloroso.”

My voice cracked. I was as frightened as I'd been in my life. I was not worried that Becky would die right there in front of me. You could tell by the way her breathing had deepened and struck a regular rhythm that she was past the danger point. I was frightened because I had no idea what to do. Part of me wanted to rush out of the door and find the nearest policeman; part of me wanted to carry Scott home where he would never be in danger again; part of me wanted to slap Becky in the face. My mind flitted back and forth through the alternatives. Then I realized part of me wanted to do all of those at once. I picked Scott up and hugged him. I couldn't think what else to do.

If it happened now, it would be the slap, no question.

An Aside on Becky's Character.

Becky was a self-destructive personality, see. (The way she'd driven her father's Edsel into the face of a gravel pit one night the summer she graduated was a metaphor for her life.) She needed to hurt herself, had to, I see now, after the beatings her father had given her as a girl discovering her sexuality, when all that hormone stuff is going on and everyone is a little crazy, some more than others. It was all about self-esteem. From those beatings Sam gave her Becky got the notion she was not a worthy person, so she went out of her way to live up to that judgment. That's what parents do to children: whatever garbage they dump on them becomes a self-fulfilling prophecy. So Becky ran around to prove to Sam Johnson she was the little bitch he claimed; and then married Hank because he was the kind of man her father despised. She was getting back at Sam, true, but more than that, she was punishing herself with Sam's rage, crying out *See, I am no good, I deserve your anger.* Oh, it was perverse, and as tangled as her taking up with Tommy Piper, knowing that Hank would find out and come after them, willing him to walk through the bedroom door and destroy her, the unworthy daughter, the fallen woman, the faithless wife. It makes perfect sense that she brought about her own death. I know it now, but back then Becky Peterson was a mystery to me, a well.

Point Number Six: One-Way Ticket to Doomsville.

She woke up suddenly. "Kelly," she said, "I've done something stupid."

"It's okay," I said.

"No," she said, "it's not." She sat up. She held out her arms and took Scott from me. "Would you get me a glass of water?" she asked. "Please."

When I came back she nodded at Scott and said, "Nothing is more important than this, right?" She hugged him and blew on his hair, teasing it up.

"I don't," he said, turning away, trying to squirm out of her grasp.

"You understand?" She'd pulled back the curtains while I was out of the room and sunlight streamed onto the bed, gold beams caught in the threads of the quilt.

"I understand," I said. I knew a mutt when I saw one.

I sat on the bed. She reached for my hand and squeezed it. She had fine bones and bird-like wrists but her grip was weak. Her hand fell away as soon as it touched mine. "It's all right," she whispered, "it won't happen again."

Scott had wriggled free of her and was bouncing on the edge of the bed. "Jump," he said, "jump me, Kelly."

"I was afraid," I said, "for the baby."

"I know." She touched my cheek. "It was stupid."

"And you. I was afraid for both of you," I lied. I picked up Scott.

"I know. It won't happen again."

I hesitated for a moment. "Scout's honour?"

"Cross my heart and hope to die."

I believed her. For Scott's sake I thought she would do whatever she had to so he was never in danger again. (Daddy always says: "You got to be tough when it gets tough.") I expected everyone lived by that code. So when Becky got up and brushed her hair and put on lipstick, I thought she had made the resolution I would have: okay, you messed up, everyone messes up now and again, but that's behind you, you have to get on with life the best you can. And that's how it seemed, too. In the days that followed she came home from work in a bustle, whisking up the walkway in her uniform, swinging her arms at her sides. She breezed about the kitchen as if everything were normal. She talked about the suppers she and Hank went to at the Flame Club. She teased me about boys: *Who's the biggest hunk?* She even brought home patterns for baby clothes and talked about sewing shirts for Scott. Becky and I told each other secrets and laughed about the ladies at church and "Pillow Talk."

"Doris Day," I said, rolling my eyes the way Becky did. "What a drip."

Becky showed me copies of *Seventeen* she'd kept in a box since she was in high school. She talked about dating tips and make-up. I brought my Everly Brothers' album over and we sang along to "Bye Bye, Love" as we washed the dishes or bathed Scott. It felt almost like sisters, sad-sack sisters.

Her mood was good, but when I reflect back now all I can think is that she was smiling on the outside while eating her heart up inside. She was terrified and alone, and I see her sitting on the end of the bed, eyes blank, hair sticking up, and I want to tear my hair out. She'd bought a one-way ticket to the graveyard, but I did not see it then and cannot go back and do anything about it now.

Extra Point: Life's Little Lessons

I learned something from Becky about that time. I learned this little lesson about life: people are going to do what they're going to do no matter what anyone else says or does to try to change their minds. I know she meant well. I know she intended to do well – if only for the sake of Scott. But good intentions do not make a lot of difference most times.

Take my grandmother, for instance. One spring she announced to the family she was staying put in her house in Winnipeg. She was in her seventies, on her own since grandpa had died a decade earlier, and my mother and aunts were concerned for her safety. She lived in a two-storey brick house. The steps up to her bedroom were narrow and steep and made of hardwood – which had worn smooth over the years. As a kid I'd fallen down them myself a couple of times when we visited her. All that spring Mother and my aunts cajoled the old lady about the house, pointing out how easy it was to slip on the stairs, how dangerous it was for her to continue living there on her own. Etcetera, etcetera. She never disagreed, just nodded and kept on with her knitting, and when all the talking was done, grandmother stayed in her house as she'd planned to all along. Of course she slipped on the stairs, fell, and broke her hip, and was hospitalized for three months, and afterwards couldn't climb stairs any more, so she had to move to a nursing home – but that's another story.

Since then I've sat with people about to do something stupid in their careers or hurtful to those they love and tried to offer reasonable advice, as we do – advice designed to make it easy for them to see their choices clearly and help them do the right thing. Usually sidestep the kind of disaster we visit upon each other and ourselves: lost jobs, broken homes, that sort of thing. They come to me looking for a sympathetic ear. And they get it. Almost always they agree with me about what I say and thank me for being such a good listener and so on. When we part they shake my hand or give me a hug. But almost always they choose the precise course of action I've counselled them not to, doing what they were going to do all along, my helpful advice a puff of smoke going up the chimney of their lives.

Point Number Seven: Booze Talking.

About a month later Becky called again sounding desperate, and that time when I ran through the front door I nearly knocked over Scott, who was on the floor playing with his toys. Thank heaven, I thought. I patted his head, kissed him quickly, and went to find Becky. She was sitting on the end of the bed. She was drinking. She had a glass filled with rum and Coke in one hand.

She popped a couple of pills into her mouth and downed them with a drink from the glass. She asked, "Want a shot?"

I looked at her, knowing she didn't mean it, and picked a few clothes off the floor. "I'll just tidy up," I said, "a little bit."

"Stop it!" she screamed at me. "Just stop it! You remind me of that idiot Tommy. Always cleaning up."

We looked at each other. "Let's not pretend," she said, "any more." She bit her lower lip and then screamed, "Tommy, Tommy, Tommy!"

"I should get the baby," I said.

"I'm depressed," she sighed. Her shoulders were slumped forward as if she were acting the part of a deranged person. Her hands trembled. (I felt the urge to take them in mine and squeeze them until they stilled.) A new bottle of pills sat open on the dresser. Dresses and skirts and blouses lay jumbled with panties and bras near the door of the closet. There were a half-dozen cigarette stubs in an ashtray, one smouldering. Becky had dumped her purse out on the top of the dresser: keys, tissues, everything. She looked awful. I found I was clenching and unclenching my fists.

By this time there were rumours around town that she went to the Flame Club without Hank and took on all comers. People knew she drank, too, and Mother said she was worried about me going to the house so often. I don't know what she imagined might happen.

Maybe that I would acquire Becky's reputation because I associated with her, a kind of emotional osmosis. She warned me one day to stop going to the Petersons' and I told her I didn't care what she and a bunch of old fart church ladies thought and she told me if I talked back one more time she'd slap my face. She said people called Becky a *tramp* and did I want to be known as one too, and I said it took one to know one and banged the screen door on the way out of the house while she was still *young-ladying* me. I thought of Becky as a friend and I thought other people should mind their own business. (When I look back now, I sometimes think I was Becky's only friend, a sixteen-year-old girl, and that says something.)

"You just need rest," I offered when she repeated she was depressed. "I'll look after Scott."

"I don't need rest," she shrieked. "I don't need rest!" She looked at the drink in her hand and then took a big swig. "Ugh," she said, "it's fizzy."

"Catalytic reaction," I said, "carbonation."

"Carbonation," she snorted. "You learn that at school?"

We were silent for a few moments, and I listened for the sounds of Scott playing, then Becky said, "I need –" She looked around the room. "I don't know what I need." It was dark in the room, an afternoon in winter. The radio was blaring away in the kitchen; strains of top forty music. Becky wore a light housecoat, her hair pinned back hastily with barrettes. Her face was ghostly in the shadows. "The doctor says I'm easily depressed."

"Everybody has bad days. Everybody is in the dumps some times."

"I wish that's all this was, I just wish, kiddo."

"My mother has them, *black days* she calls them. Stay out of her way then, she's Warpath Wilma." I tried to laugh. I was standing in the doorway, clenching my fists. I wanted to cross the room and throw my arms around Becky's thin shoulders. Either that or slap her face so she'd snap out of it.

"I don't know what to think."

"Think of Scott."

"Go on." She sniffed and shook her head. "Get the hell out of here."

"Come on, Becky, everybody gets down."

"You bet," she said. She sighed, and I thought that meant she agreed with me, but she stood suddenly and screamed, "Do they do this?"

She flung the half-filled tumbler against the wall opposite. It smashed and broken glass fell to the floor. "Or this?" She picked a framed picture off the bedside table and smashed it down on the edge of the dresser. Then she raised one of her tiny fists and bashed it against the plaster wall. "Or this?" she sobbed, "or this," smashing her fist against the wall until the window panes rattled and her knuckles were scraped and blood ran down her wrist.

I had backed away from her. Oddly, I was thinking about Scott. If you left him alone he'd put things in his mouth, or crawl down the basement stairs. He'd fallen once and scraped the skin off his nose. My mind was still on him, but it was reeling, too, I had no idea what Becky might do next. I thought she had been fooling about being depressive – not fooling but exaggerating the way girls did when they said they'd kill themselves if some boy asked them to the dance – but I saw she wasn't. This was what depressive meant, really meant.

I stumbled in my haste to back away from her.

"Don't go," Becky pleaded. She let her hand fall onto the dresser top, where it rested among the jumbled contents of her purse, bleeding into the keys and tissues. "Don't leave."

"What about the baby?"

"The baby?" she screamed, angry again. "Why is everyone only worried about the goddamn baby?" She banged both hands on the dresser top. "The goddamn baby."

"They're not," I said. "Not really."

"God," she said. "What I'd give for one day, just one day…." She sat suddenly on the end of the bed and buried her face in her hands. Out in the hallway Scott was playing with his cars, crashing them into each other. I heard him laughing to himself. In a minute he was in the doorway, a green cement truck in one hand, a red fire engine in the other.

"Mommy sad," he said. He reached his hands out to me.

"Yes," I whispered. "Hush now."

"I'm crashing," he said. "Come and see, Kelly."

"Okay," I said. "I'll be there in a moment. One teensy."

"Come and see now," he said.

"Honey," I said, "why don't you get a candy from the red dish?"

"Yeah," he said. "Cangy."

When he scuttled off, Becky sighed audibly and said, "I'm not really the wreck it seems." She was sitting up again, running her hands through her hair. Light from the overhead fixture shone on her head. She was wrong. Only the *Titanic* was in her league.

I was wondering if Scott would tip the candy dish over and make a mess on the living-room carpet. I heard him moving about, bumping into chairs.

Becky said, "It just gets the better of me sometimes." We were silent for a moment. I heard the radio again. "Devoted To You." What a joke.

When I didn't say anything, Becky added, "Hank, the baby, everything about this godforsaken dump of a town." She stood and picked up the bottle of pills, and then shook two into her hand and swallowed them in one gulp.

I reached over and laid my hand on her arm. "Maybe," I said, "that's not such a great idea. Popping all those pills."

"Don't you start," she said.

"I was thinking of the baby."

"I know what's on your mind." She pushed my hand away. "Don't I just, kiddo, I've watched you looking at Hank."

It was such an illogical thing to say I started to laugh.

"You're not fooling me," she said.

I choked out, "Don't be ridiculous."

"I know those tricks."

"I'm going," I said. "I won't hear any more of this. Accusations."

"I know those tricks from the inside out," she shouted. "Making eyes at married men. Wiggling your little tail."

"You're crazy. And you're drunk. Drunk as a camel."

"Leering at him, wearing those angora sweaters over here."

"For God's sake, Becky," I said, "just shut it, will you?"

"You like the idea, is that it, what goes on between the sheets?"

"If I wanted to – to look – at Hank I'd encourage you to *take* pills. Jesus."

"Not you," she said. "You're devious."

Takes one to know one, I thought, but I bit my lip and let it go. I went to find the baby and when I did I had to pick a dozen round candies off the carpet and wipe away the syrupy smear he'd made of his mouth. He had his rubber ball in one hand so we rolled that back and forth on the kitchen floor while I sniffled back sobs and thought of mean things to say to Becky. My heart was thumping and I had to keep swallowing hard over and over again. Then I fixed Scott a bowl of cereal with milk. The afternoon was a good time of day for him: unlike a lot of kids who got tired and cranky as the day wore on, he was filled with energy and wanted to be playing. He was just finishing his cereal when Becky appeared in a navy jumper, the kind the girls at the Catholic school wore. She leaned against the kitchen counter, smoking and watching us play.

"Look at this, Mommy," Scott said, as he rolled the ball directly into my hands. Becky reached down and ruffled his hair.

"Look at that," I said. "What a clever boy."

"He is, isn't he?"

"He's the sugar in our tea."

After a while Becky said, "You won't hold it against me, will you?"

I said to Scott, "Roll one to Mommy. That's a good boy."

He bounced the ball over her toes. It spun for a moment, then lay inert.

"Kelly?"

"No," I said. "I won't."

"It was the booze talking. I know you and Hank, that's – that's nuts."

"You got that right, kiddo."

"That's nuts." She held her hands crossed over her belly. She had washed the blood off her wrist.

"It damn well is, yes," I said.

"It was the booze," she said. "How ridiculous to say that."

"You're like another person sometimes, Becky, I don't know you."

The afternoon had worn on and the light coming in the window was faint, just a glaze on the patchy pallor of Becky's skin. She poured a glass of water and drank it while I retrieved the ball and rolled it to Scott. She told me Hank was out at the arena with the team and asked if I knew any of the boys. Yes, I said: Andy Buechler who lived next door, and Phil Boileau, the goalie, and Gordon McCabe. I had a crush on Gordon and when I said his name I felt myself blush. He had dark hair and blue eyes and was a good dancer, better than Andy for sure, but not as smart. They all thought Hank was a great coach, I told her.

"Yeah," she said.

"But he loses it sometimes, you know, flips out. Hurricane Hank."

"Yeah. He can have a temper."

"Once he hit Randy. Randy was laughing or something after Hank had told them to stop. He was trying to explain something. When Randy laughed in his face Hank hit him or something. All the guys forgave him right away, of course. You know Randy, he's a mug, he deserved it."

"Yeah," Becky said, "but he does have that temper." She coughed into her hand. "He's never raised a hand to Scott."

"No, of course."

Becky asked if I was in the play at school. A small part, I said, because there weren't many roles for girls in *Romeo and Juliet,* and Linda Simpson had the lead. Becky wanted to know, was she the most popular in the class? The smartest, I said. The most popular was Pam Sinclair, Pammy the Pill. Weren't they all, I said, the popular girls. *Witches and bitches,* I said. Becky bit her lip and lighted a cigarette. And how was my mother, she wanted to know, and my father?

It was obvious she was leading up to something. They were fine, both of them. Daddy had built a rock fence down one side of the yard and Mother was making pedal pushers from patterns.

Becky grunted. She asked me if I'd like some juice and after we'd both had a drink she said, casually, "You won't tell anyone will you?"

I looked at her then, for the space of a long count of ten. I had never seen an adult really afraid of me and I made a mental note of where the fear was most evident: in the way she wrung her hands together, fingers trembling with every breath. It was electric, sensing the thrill of power, as much a charge as when I'd said that popular girls were witches and bitches, knowing Becky had been the most popular in her class and seeing her flinch. I wanted to hurt her after what she'd said about me and Hank, and I did it just by saying a few words. But I'd become a toad for a moment there, and that hurt, too.

"No," I said, "I won't tell."

"I love him," she said. "He's all that matters."

She meant Scott, and I knew in that moment she believed it. I don't think I did. (Love was something much more grand to me, then, more thrilling.) But something else was true, Scott needed her, and that's what I was going on, need, not love. You could see it in the way he clung to her leg when she left for work and the way he leapt from his toys when he heard her open the door. *My mommy.* It wasn't right that a beautiful child should be so attached to such a mother, but what did that signify? (Another of

Daddy's favourite sayings: No one claimed life was going to be fair.)

"Don't worry," I said. "I won't rat on you."

Becky shivered dramatically and blew her cheeks out, like a horse, and then she finished her juice and started to fix supper. She took two pork chops out of the fridge and put potatoes in a pot. "You know," she said, "I shouldn't tell you this, but he hits me." She stood at the sink, running water over the potatoes while scrubbing off loose skin with a wire brush. I rolled the ball back and forth with Scott. By mutual consent we did not look at each other, something I had learned from Mother when we talked about touchy subjects. "That time in the spring when my chin was puffed up and I said I'd fallen down the stairs?" Becky's voice had gone quite still. I listened to the brush scraping the sides of the pot, to the squeak of Scott's shoes on the linoleum. "Other times too. I don't know what brings the anger on. He's not jealous."

Becky was capable of all kinds of deception, self-deception included, so I don't think I believed her, but I said, "If that happened to me, I'd go."

"You'd what?"

"Leave. Take the baby and get out of here. Pronto."

"Kelly," she said, "don't be ridiculous."

"I'm not being ridiculous," I said.

"Leave? This is my home, Red Rock."

"It wouldn't matter. I wouldn't let any man do that to me. Not even once." I had finished drinking and I reached the juice glass up to the counter without looking at her.

"How old are you?"

"Age," I said, "has nothing to do with it."

"You're very sure of yourself, you know. For a girl who –"

"It's disgusting," I said. "And no one should put up with it."

"They do, kiddo. *We* do."

"I wouldn't."

Becky turned at the counter, and when she did I looked up into her face. There was a tiny fan of creases in the corner of her eyes, much smaller than Mother's, but you could read in them the woman she would become in middle age, sharpish features, if well-preserved. Tough. She said, "No, I can see that. I can see you wouldn't put up with much." She placed the pot of potatoes on the stove top and switched on the element. She sighed. "That's good, too," she said in a whisper. "I wish more women were that strong. I wish I was."

"Don't let yourself off the hook that way. You can be what you want."

"Kelly, you have no idea –"

"It's what you said before, about not getting walked on. Doormats."

She looked at me again. "*You* said that."

"You agreed."

"We were talking about something else. Entirely. Christ."

"You're damn right. About using anger."

"No," she said.

"About using what's in your guts to say *don't walk all over me.* Jesus."

"No!" she shouted. "No, no, no!" She banged her open palm on the counter and the dishes rattled in the cupboard and Scott looked up from our game, startled.

He said, "I'm scared." He put out his hands and I held one in mine.

"It's okay," I said. "Mommy's just –"

"What you don't get is how ridiculous you sound, a girl in bobby socks, telling a grown woman how to behave."

"I'm no mutt. And I know what I would take and what I wouldn't."

"You know nothing of the kind. You've never done anything, you've never been any place. All you've ever done is read books."

"That's a cheap thing to say. From someone who hasn't."

"You're just a kid with big ideas."

"At least I have an idea. At least I think."

"You're just a little – a little virgin with her legs still crossed."

"And you're, you're a –"

"Go on, say it." (We were staring each other in the eye, me looking up and she looking down, hate for hate.) "Say it," she hissed through gritted teeth, "and I'll slap your face for you when you do."

If she hadn't challenged me I wouldn't have said it, and when I did, her hand flicked out to my cheek, as she'd threatened, and touched it like a kiss, and I heard flesh smack flesh and felt the sting and heard her gasp – and then we were sitting on the floor hugging and Scott was hugging us too and saying, "Kelly hurt," and we were all three crying.

"What you don't get," Becky choked through tears, "is that you're the oddball, not the rest of us. You with your ridiculous ideas."

I was stroking Scott's hair with one hand and pounding the floor with the other, balled into a fist. "The hell with you, Becky, the hell with all of you."

Becky snorted. "Oh, wise up," she said. I felt the pounding of her chest against mine. After a moment she asked, "How many girls in your class have been, you know, molested?" She glanced at Scott and then added, "Forced?" She drew back and looked me in the eye. "Go on," she said, "tell me. And while you're at it, include me. Yeah. And consider this: how many girls have to get married every year? *Up the stump,* whatever the current expression." When I didn't answer she said, "You're right, numbers don't matter. What matters is we're trapped, and most us don't even know we're trapped."

"That's sad."

"It's true. It turns some of us into witches and the rest into – into sluts."

"I didn't mean that."

"It doesn't matter. The point is we're all trash. One way or the other."

"I didn't mean it, Becky. Jesus."

"It's the truth, kiddo. We're either playthings or

pieces of trash."

"It's pathetic."

"Pills, drinking, whoring around. We all do something to get back."

"It doesn't have to be."

"You believe you can get what you want, that's your problem, kiddo."

"My father says you have to. Do for yourself, he says."

"Now I've heard everything." Becky breathed into the nape of my neck for a minute, a mixture of warmth and damp I remembered from the caresses Mother gave me before bed, the next best thing to falling asleep in the back seat of the car under the old army blanket, Daddy and Mother talking up front. Then Becky gave me a quick hug and stood up. "Most of us," she said, "take what's given."

The girls at school said that too, except not in those words. The more ambitious among us talked about going to nursing school in Port Arthur and some to teachers' college, but they were in the minority. (A few like Janet and me had secret ambitions, hers to be a vet up north and mine to practise law in Toronto: according to Daddy I had the gift of the gab.) Most girls knew that homes and babies were all that awaited them when they were finished school, and that was what they were settling for. Settling. They were hoping to marry one of the nicer boys, one who was good-looking and would buy them a new house and take them on trips in the summer to the Rockies and not drink too much and carry on.

The problem for Becky was she'd started out in the first group and ended up in the second.

She said, "Hank's not a bad man."

"No," I said.

"He loves Scottie." She was stroking the back of her injured hand now, massaging it.

"He does."

She smiled. "He touches him all the time."

"He does," I whispered. I'd watched him stroking Scott's hair, which was thin, dark, and wispy. Hank was a man who touched people, but it wasn't always with the tenderness he showed his child.

Point Number Eight: Confession.

Despite what Becky had hinted, no man had ever touched me. I had heard the girls at school whispering about the janitor once, a swarthy young guy from Portugal with a pencil moustache who was supposed to have taken Rowena Backstrom into the basement and lifted her skirt, and our mothers were always warning us about Tommy Piper giving girls rides home in his flashy car, but we were very wary of anyone other than the boys in school.

I had heard men talk, however.

Every year my parents had two big parties in the house, one at their anniversary in October and the other to celebrate New Year. The house was filled with people, my parents' married friends and a few younger couples they knew from church or work. They spent most of the evening in the basement, where they danced and drank, the men beer, the women lemon gin with 7-Up. From time to time groups formed somewhere to talk, women in the kitchen, men round the dart board in one corner of the basement. I was allowed to prowl around, picking up empties and putting out plates of sandwiches. (Seen but not heard, according to Daddy.)

But I listened. The women whispered about girls who were pregnant, *in trouble,* they said, and couples whose marriages were coming apart, *on the rocks*. They talked about who was going where for summer vacation and who was carrying on with whom and who was dying of what, their hushed voices dropping suddenly if it was someone they knew. *Poor Maddy, two babies, the cervix.* They touched their painted nails to their mouths and shook their heads and sipped their lemon gins. (I tried pursing my mouth the way Mrs. Buechler did, sticking out my lower lip like the Grouper fish in the aquarium at school. I had to suppress my laughter and flee to the basement.) The men stood near the counter where Daddy kept the darts, drinking beer from the bottle. They wore white shirts with sleeves rolled to the elbow, and ties they'd loosened round their necks. Their talk was about women too. Who looked good in shorts at the church picnic, who had hot pants, who you'd put the blocks to if you got the chance – Pammy Sinclair, apparently, she gave the young guys blue balls. I crouched behind the counter at the far end of the room, holding my stomach, wishing I was still upstairs, where the women were talking about tumours and pregnancy. I didn't want to but I listened to the ugly words, *big knockers, box, bang,* until my face was hot and my back hurt from crouching. I was surprised by some of the voices I heard: Doctor Tom McCabe, Roy Buechler, Chief Dixon. (I did not hear Daddy's and I felt good about that.)

I think if Hank Peterson had been there he might have joined in, but I do not know for certain. He was not shy when it came to women. If we stood talking in the kitchen about Scott while waiting for Becky to finish dressing he stroked my shoulder, and when we walked down the hall he'd place one hand in the middle of my back, guiding me, the fingers lightly fondling my spine and rib cage in rhythm with our voices. Not exactly creepy but in the zone. His breath smelled of mints when he bent over to whisper in my ear. The hair on the back of my neck stood up, shivers. Hank was dangerous.

I only saw him mad once. It was in July and he'd planted about half the spruces along the back of the yard. (He was making a double row in case some died.) It started raining one weekend and kept on into the middle of the next week, unusual for Red Rock, where we got thunderstorms all the time but not continuous rain. Hank fussed and fumed and stared out the windows at the rain as if that would make it go away. He liked the routine of coming home and working in the yard – or going to the ball field, one or the other. The rain put a stop to both. He had to spend evenings inside, where he couldn't run and play with Scott, even.

From what Becky told me, he prowled the house when I wasn't there, too, making a nuisance of himself and being short-tempered with the baby. The rain stopped for a day or two, just enough for the ground to dry some, but not enough for him to be able to dig in it, and then it started up again for two or three more days. Hank stormed and brooded. This kept on for a couple of weeks, every day looking as if it might be the end of the rain, only to bring showers about dinner time. Daddy was in a state himself. Gordon and Andy and the guys on the baseball team were cranky when you ran into them at The Steep Rock Café having Cokes.

One day Hank came home from afternoon shift. It had been sunny since noon, the unusual light that comes after days of rain tingeing the houses with a pink glow. I'd had Scott out riding his tricycle on the sidewalk. Hank drove up, waved, and bounded up the steps into the house, Scott right behind him: *my daddy, my daddy.* Just about the time Hank came out again, carrying his work gloves, I heard the first clap of thunder. "Good Christ," Hank muttered. He slapped his gloves together in one palm and glared at the sky. He stood in the yard, watching the sky turn black as the clouds rolled in. It took about an hour. He had a shovel in one hand and he banged it on top of the picnic table. When the rain really got going he leapt onto the picnic table and jumped up and down, beating the shovel on the wood until chips flew off it. After, he sat on the steps in the rain, his khaki work shirt soaked through, and then he came inside. *Don't come near me,* he whispered in a gravelly voice, *just don't dare.*

Point The Last: Tragedy

By the time I got to the Petersons' the Friday morning of the shootings, Hank was already inside the house. Someone said he had just sat on the steps looking dazed until Dixon took him inside. *Stunned,* someone whispered, like it wasn't him who'd done anything. The Johnsons were expected any minute, somebody else said, and Mrs. Buechler had carried the baby into her house. I watched the windows of the Buechlers' but I didn't see anybody, not even the girls at the windows, who Janet had spotted earlier. We stood out there in the cold morning air for some time, talking in subdued voices, as people do after disasters, *tut-tutting* and *isn't-that-so-ing,* but secretly feeling relieved it wasn't them got flooded out or whatever. (Another of Daddy's sayings: Better you than me.) Andy's dad was there for a while, and Mr. Butler, whose glances towards Jonathan Morris were so pointed he would have given them away if the Mom Brigade had not already made them as hot a topic of gossip as Becky and Tommy. Small towns. (As Daddy said, Roy Buechler was not the only one in Red Rock washing his neighbours' underwear.)

The Head Mom, mine, came over after a while. She was wearing a pair of pedal pushers and had put on lipstick. She stood with Madelaine Russell, conferring in whispers and glancing at me from time to time. There weren't many fathers there. Daddy was on days that week. Most of the men in the neighbourhood must have been. Women slipped from one knot of observers to another, gathering information and clucking tongues. Mother sidled up to me. "I won't say I told you so," she whispered.

Typical, I thought. I blew on my fingers.

"They say they're both dead," Mother whispered. "Stone dead."

"Do they," I said. I studied the windows of the Petersons' house, where the sun was making discs of silvery light on the glazed glass.

"They say Becky is already gone, that's why they haven't brought her out on the stretcher."

She rubbed her thumb and index finger against the corners of her mouth waiting for me to answer, but I refused to look her way. Instead I studied the sky, which was a washed-out tint of pink, mixed with greys.

"Well," she added, "it's a shame in one way."

"I wonder." I rubbed my hands together, feeling the stiffness at the ends of my fingers and then muttered, "I wonder what that way would be."

We stood in silence for a minute and then Mother finally said, "Penny for your thoughts."

"I was wondering about Scott," I said. It was a lie. I was calculating how long it would be before I could leave Red Rock. I'd thought I liked the small town atmosphere, the know-all-about-everyone-else coziness, but there in the pale light of dawn I decided to skip grade thirteen and make it up at the university. You could do that, Daddy had told me. (Just clear the hell off, he would have said.) I was sick of iron ore and The Steep Rock Café and small town gossip.

"It's always the children," Mother said, "who suffer."

"Scott will be okay," I said. At the Buechlers' the lights were on. It looked warm inside. I wondered if they were having breakfast, giving Scott cereal with milk. He liked corn flakes but not porridge. Mother cleared her throat.

"Maddy says there was blood all over the bedroom. Walls too. Bloody as a slaughterhouse."

I asked, "How could she know that?"

"Lyle Butler," Mother said. "Maddy says he says it was a shotgun Hank used."

"Is that what she says?"

"It is. A twelve gauge. Whatever that means."

"He should have strangled them both in bed, a man with Hank's hands."

Mother looked at me. "You scare me sometimes," she said. "I never know what's going on in that head of yours."

I hugged my arms across my chest. "In any case," I said, "they make a lot of noise, shotguns."

"I heard it," Mother said. *"Wham, wham.* Maddy says the first one rattled dishes in the cupboard, she jumped up to see if any were broken, and when the second one came she thought their kitchen clock was going to fall off the wall."

I grunted. I thought of Mrs. Russell drinking her morning coffee and making a note of how the vibrations shook her kitchen things. I had thought the two shots occurred one right after the other, but I realized then there had been time enough for Mrs. Russell to get up and look in her cupboards before the second shot was fired. I wondered what Becky and Hank were doing during that time and I closed my mind against the thought. I believe now that whatever passed between them was the most significant thing that occurred in their brief and hopeless lives, a kind of epiphany in which all the bad things they had done suddenly made sense. (The Big Reckoning, you could call it, where they saw each other for what they were and forgave all.)

Mother said, "Hank marched into the bedroom and let them have it."

"Huh."

"Killed them both. Cold blood."

"Is that so?"

"It *was* a shotgun. Maddy saw Dixon put it in the cruiser car."

"I saw that too. In the trunk."

"Yes," Mother said. "He locked the gun away for evidence. We all saw that." She blew on her fingers. I noticed they were cracked and chafed, and then she asked, "So what's with you, then?"

"Nothing, Mother." I had come out in my sneakers, and the damp and cold had were turning my feet to ice. I rubbed one toe on top of the other to increase circulation.

"Kelly," Mother said. "What?"

"Nothing. For God's sake, Mother, nothing, nothing, nothing."

Mother said, "I don't know why, Kelly, you always have to pretend to know more than you do. Rolling your eyes, taking that high and mighty tone. Is this some phase you're going through? Something you picked up at school – or from Becky?"

"It is not a phase."

"You're so – so bloody independent."

"You may recall, Mother, you came over here digging for dirt."

"Dirt," she said. "I like that. These are our neighbours."

"Dirt, Mother. It makes whoever is digging for it *dirty.*"

Mother blinked. "I take an interest."

"Call it what you will. It's sordid and sleazy. I'm not interested."

"You don't know anything, is more like it." She gave me one of her looks, then glanced across to Madelaine Russell and shrugged her shoulders.

"Have it your way," I said. "I don't give a good God damn."

"Kelly." Mother's voice was a hoarse whisper. She tugged my sleeve.

"Let go, Mother, for Christ's sake."

"People will hear you."

"I don't give a shit if they do."

She glared at me. "Watch your tongue, young lady."

"Let go Mother," I said. "Right now, or by the Christ –"

"I don't know what's got into you," Mother hissed. "I can't even talk to you." She sniffed, then turned her face one way and I turned in the other. Most of the crowd had dispersed, mothers gathering their families together and heading back to their warm homes. It was cold and there was nothing to see. Soon the kids would be off to school, getting books sorted and lunch kits. It seemed to me classes would be even more pointless than usual, but what could you do? We were silent for a minute or two and then Mother said, "It was just a civil question."

"I care, Mother," I hissed back, "which is more than I can say for you and all the Madelaine Russells in Red Rock put together."

"Give me strength."

"About something worth caring for."

"Oh, you are something," Mother said. "A real case. A real odd one."

We stood silently for a few moments and then she said, "Just because Becky liked listening to the Everly Brothers. You have to take her side."

"That's what I mean. The Everly Brothers were not her style. She –"

"You know what I mean."

"I know you're jealous of her."

"That does take the cake. Me?"

I snorted but held my tongue.

We stood in silence watching Chief Dixon and Hank through the living-room window of the Petersons', Mother scratching at her chafed fingers and me hugging my arms across my chest. Hank sat on the sofa facing into the house. All we could see of him was the back of his head, hair standing straight up. Dixon moved from room to room, carrying things and speaking to Hank, it seemed. Then he noticed the curtains were open and he pulled them shut and we had nothing to look at.

"It doesn't make sense," Mother said.

"No," I said. "It doesn't."

She shook her head and paced to and fro. "It just doesn't make sense."

She looked at me, waiting for an explanation, but I shrugged. The truth of it was she was right, but that was not good enough for her. Mother needed things to add up. Becky having the hots for Tommy but staying with Hank, Hank blasting away with a shotgun at his wife, those things did not add up. There was not sufficient logic there for Mother. In her world, the world of the church – the sacraments, rituals, ordered events – life made sense. Everything, good or bad, had a reason in Mother's world, some sort of logical progression to it that you could sit down and explain to yourself and your kids. First this, and then that. You know, order. In that world women did not die without an explanation and children did not suffer. Even the fall of a sparrow could be accounted for. She could not get her head around the idea that life was maybe a jigsaw with one piece missing, a deck of fifty-one cards.

"She was so young," Mother said finally. "Such a good-looking girl."

"Woman."

"That's what I said." Mother studied her hands. "Hank too," she said. "Both so good-looking."

"Is that the measure of a tragedy – whether whoever died was attractive?"

Mother sighed. "You worry me, young lady, you know that?"

"It'll be all right," I said.

"You think?" Mother sniffed and rubbed the end of her nose. Then she said, "There's so much suffering in this life."

"Whatever happens, Mother, happens. So it has to be okay. Right?"

Mother looked at me. "Sometimes," she sighed, "I haven't the foggiest idea what you're talking about."

"Que sera, sera."

"Really." Mother shook her head. "Not the foggiest."

"I thought that was your favourite song? Doris the Dip."

Mother groaned. After a while she said, "I'm going." And when I didn't answer, she said, "You too."

"In a minute," I said.

"Right away." She gave me her exasperated mother sigh and strode off.

I've wondered since how much she really knew about Hank and Becky. In the years that passed she spoke of them very little and I had the impression there was something about what had happened to them that touched a place in her too deep to acknowledge. Maybe she identified with Becky in some way I could not perceive. Maybe, like most women, her insides revolted at the idea that a man could do that to his wife. Or maybe she didn't want to consider the other explanations of Becky's death.

In a little while the Johnsons arrived in their yellow Edsel. He got out first and walked around to the other side of the car and opened the door for her. She was wearing a head scarf and a heavy black coat, Persian wool, Mother had been eyeing one in the Eaton's catalogue and had been hoping Father would get the hint at Christmas. Mrs. Johnson had difficulty standing and Mr. Johnson gave her his arm when she staggered getting out, and closed the car door while she stood to one side, looking dazed. What was left of the crowd fell silent. I felt a lump rise in my throat. A number of people coughed. Everyone knew the Johnsons and how they thought themselves a little too good for Red Rock, but that morning everybody standing on the sidewalk in front of Hank and Becky's was surely thinking, as I was, there go Becky's parents, who gave their child the best they could and took her to church and sniffed with her over skinned knees and bad report cards and sighed with relief the night Tommy drove into Dead Man's Curve and it was not their girl in the car, too. They were an older couple, in their late fifties and they did not deserve to be burying their child, no parent deserved that, it was against the natural order of things, and yet there they were, making their way to the Buechlers' front door to greet their grandson, now their son, who one day soon they would be in charge of raising and on another, mercifully distant day, have to explain Becky's death to. I stuck my chin down into my sweater thinking about that and swallowed back a lump about as big as a bowling ball.

Since then I've sat in my office in what one wag once called Shrinks' Row (I became a psychiatrist, not a lawyer), and I've thought of that moment a lot, and what comes back to me is how frail the Johnsons looked getting out of their car. Defeated by Becky's death. And yet in one important sense they were responsible for it, and for the whole rotten tragedy.

What did they tell Scott? Platitudes, most likely, things to make him feel good and remember his mother in the best light. Lies, in other words – and I do not know if anyone would have done otherwise.

But now I know what they should have told him but could not have even if they'd known it themselves, because it would have meant admitting Becky's final moments were no more than retaliation against them. She was not strong, I see that now, though she was a tough little article, tough on the outside. So at the last moment she was hoping that death would free her from what she could not escape in life. She may have pulled the trigger herself.

I have difficulty imagining that. I have difficulty imagining her peering down the barrel of the shotgun and then pulling the trigger, though I do not have trouble with the abstract idea that Becky could have killed herself. I can't see Hank doing it either, no matter how often the high school guys, Andy and Gordon included, insisted Hank knew guns and had every reason and the like. He was not a killer. (I've seen them since and they've all got something in the eyes, some day we'll be able to measure it, I'm sure, and we'll look back at our ignorance now and find it as amusing as leeching.) Hank didn't have that look. And as the years have spun out I've grown more sure of his innocence, though I'm probably in the minority, given what people like Chief Dixon were always ready to say and the blank look that came over

Andy's face if you mentioned how sad it was Hank had to leave Red Rock. He was not alone. A general uneasiness about Hank Peterson pervaded Red Rock, and indeed you could almost hear the collective sigh of relief when he left. People had been holding their breath, half hoping he would make a clean breast of it and terrified that he would.

As it was Hank kept silent during the trial. (He was that kind of guy, the kind to take it to the grave in silence, the kind to do the honourable thing.) So despite the claims and counterclaims – the finger prints, the blood samples, the photographs – Hank was silent, his way of loving Becky to the end. (I wonder what she thought of that, as she looked down from the clouds or whatever shadows the dead retreat to.)

The lawyers had a field day. By the time they came to their summing-up speeches, the whole episode was a snarl of half-truths and guesses and details that didn't add up. Not if you considered only the facts. But when you think of things now in the cold light of day, the man Hank was, the woman Becky had become, her death makes sense in a perverse way.

There was a photograph of her in the paper about a year later, not one of the sensational ones from the time of the trial, but earlier, and what struck me is how young she was. They all were, all three of them barely out of high school and yet up to their necks in stupidity and mayhem, as Daddy would have said. There were at least four lives ruined there, and plenty more sobered and saddened. That nothing can change. All our lives grew darker from that morning onward. So in a way it doesn't matter how Becky died – who really killed her, I mean – though it's frustrating not to know, really know, after all these years.

Suddenly in December, Hank was free to walk the streets of Red Rock again. The trial had taken nearly a month, but the jury needed only an hour and a half to reach their verdict, and they felt along with most of us in town that Hank had suffered enough by then and that Scott needed at least one parent if he was going to make it in this life. That anyway was a positive: father and son together.

They stopped by my parents' house, the two of them in the car, on their way out of Red Rock one morning in the year I myself left for this city and the life I now lead. It was spring, then, a thin light was coming in over the tree tops, a good light that says winter has passed. Hank was pale and nervous. He couldn't look me in the eye. It broke my heart to see Scott in the front seat, surrounded by his Tinker Toys, the same toys we'd played with on the floor of the Johnsons' living-room the past three or four months. I knew I'd never see him again. He smiled after I kissed his cheek and he said *teeny hugs,* and I gave him the Teddy bear I'd kept at the foot of my bed through my childhood and he smiled again through the car window, and then they were gone, the red dust billowing up behind Hank's Meteor as they drove down the street and over the Pickerel River.

WAYNE TEFS is an award-winning Winnipeg fiction writer and editor. *Red Rock: A Mystery* is his sixth novel. "Red Rock and After," the short story on which this novel is based, was a winner of the Western Magazine Awards Fiction Prize, and a finalist for the Journey Prize. His work has been shortlisted for several CBC Literary Competitions, the Books in Canada First Novel Award and the Seal Book Prize. His numerous short stories have been published in literary periodicals.

Wayne Tefs was born in St. Boniface, and educated at the University of Manitoba and the University of Toronto. A recipient of the Woodrow Wilson Fellowship, he has taught at a number of colleges and universities. He lives in Winnipeg with his wife and son.

OTHER NOVELS BY WAYNE TEFS

Figures On A Wharf

The Cartier Street Contract

The Canasta Players

Dickie

Home Free